"You're not... I've seen nu...

Brenna's exasp... voice as she called to Trip through the locked bathroom door. "For heaven's sake, we're both doctors. Trust me!"

Trip opened the door a crack. "If you're so trustworthy, put your money where your mouth is."

"How?"

"Drop your nightie and show me *your* stuff without a blush."

Brenna tightened the belt on her robe. "I'm not the one who can't get dressed alone because of a couple of casts and a bruised set of ribs. And I'm not about to drop my nightgown just so we can be twinsies when I tuck you back in bed."

"Who says you're tucking me in?"

"If you can't get *out* of bed without me, you can't get back *in* without me." Brenna realized her slip immediately. "You know what I mean . . ."

"Sure I do, Brenna." Trip's eyes were sparkling as he played his advantage. "You're *welcome* in my bed anytime . . ."

The Magic Touch

ROSEANNE WILLIAMS

MILLS & BOON LIMITED
ETON HOUSE, 18-24 PARADISE ROAD
RICHMOND, SURREY TW9 1SR

All the characters in this book have no existence outside the imagination of the Author, and have no relation whatsoever to anyone bearing the same name or names. They are not even distantly inspired by any individual known or unknown to the Author, and all the incidents are pure invention.

All rights reserved. The text of this publication or any part thereof may not be reproduced or transmitted in any form or by any means, electronic or mechanical, including photocopying, recording, storage in an information retrieval system, or otherwise, without the written permission of the publisher.

This book is sold subject to the condition that it shall not, by way of trade or otherwise, be lent, resold, hired out or otherwise circulated without the prior consent of the publisher in any form of binding or cover other than that in which it is published and without a similar condition including this condition being imposed on the subsequent purchaser.

*First published in Great Britain in 1991
by Mills & Boon Limited, Eton House, 18-24 Paradise Road,
Richmond, Surrey TW9 1SR*

© Sheila Slattery 1990

ISBN 0 263 77350 7

21 – 9105

Made and printed in Great Britain

1

BRENNA DEVENEY HAD BEGUN to doubt her road map, as well as the wisdom of doing long-distance veterinary relief work, when a weathered sign ahead removed one doubt.

Hart Ranch, Tristan Perez Hart, Veterinarian, it read.

This was it, Trip Hart's place. Blessing the map, still dubious of her wisdom, Brenna turned onto a long gravel driveway that led to the sprawling California ranch house Lita Hart had described to her over the phone. What drew Brenna's immediate attention and held it, however, was the other landmark Mrs. Hart had described—the devastation from last week's bushfire.

Brenna braked near the end of the driveway, riveted by the charred swath that branded the backdrop of golden hills framing the house. Somewhere up there, Trip had been felled by a scorched oak tree in an attempt to save a lame deer from the raging fire. Trip now lay in a hospital a hundred miles away with multiple injuries.

Brenna grimaced, then switched her focus to the back seat where Byron and Malia begged to get out. "Not yet." She sighed and got out of the car. The front screen door of the house opened before she reached the porch. Shading her eyes against the scorching glare of the sun, she said, "Hi. I'm Brenna, the relief veterinarian from San Jose."

Smiling broadly, Carmelita Perez Hart stepped down from the shade of the porch and shook Brenna's hand.

"*Buenos días*, Brenna. I'm Lita. How was your drive over?"

"Not bad. I made it in just under two hours." Brenna tucked one side of her light brown chin-length bob behind her ear and tried not to stare at Trip Hart's mother.

Lita was not at all the matronly office receptionist Brenna had visualized from her phone call. Except for a bandaged wrist in a shoulder sling, she resembled nothing so much as a slim, sixty-year-old version of a sixties folksinger. Wearing jeans, with her silvered black hair in a braid to her waist and big silver hoops in her pierced ears, she radiated the image and energy of a much younger woman.

"*Gracias* for coming out on such short notice. We need you, *amiga*."

"I'm ready to dig in."

"Dig in after you get unpacked and have lunch," said Lita. "I hope you like vegetarian tamales."

"Lead me to them."

Lita laughed. "That's what Trip always says when the subject is tamales, burritos or enchiladas."

"How is he?"

Lita's smile clouded. "The doctors have decided he—" She bit her lip and tears misted in her dark eyes. "He'll never use his left leg again. His right hand and forearm—only partial use, if he's lucky. He has a concussion, bruised ribs." She pulled in a deep breath. "As I said when I called, I don't know how long we'll need you—at least until he's out of the hospital and decides what to do with his practice. I wish I could be more specific."

"No problem. I can work as long as necessary," Brenna assured her. "I came prepared for an extended stay, and

I can drive back later in the week to pick up anything else I might need."

"*Bueno.* You'll have a free hand here, Brenna. Trip's truck is yours to use for field calls. I told him I'm leaving everything to you, and I've forbidden him to even ask how things are going here until he's out of the hospital. I promised him his practice would stay on an even keel until he's back. If it turns out he can continue doing surgery, all won't be lost. If he can't though . . ."

"I'll hope for the best, too," Brenna said quickly as Lita's tears threatened to spill over. To give his mother a moment to compose herself, she turned to survey the surrounding oak-studded hills and wondered if she'd made a mistake in coming so far afield to do relief work.

Maybe not. There was peace here, simplicity, natural beauty. She needed that right now. A place to heal completely from being denied the clinic partnership she had wanted so badly after six years of dedicated veterinary work. A place to decide what to do now that she wouldn't be following the career path she had laid out for herself.

"This is beautiful country," she said, to block the painful rush of memory. "I've never spent any time in the central coast range before. It's so . . ."

"Beautiful but isolated?" Lita supplied, her dark eyes clearing. "It's both at the same time, but don't let these hills fool you, Doctor. They're rich with California history. And there are ranches of every size up here with enough animals, large and small, to keep a good vet busy."

Brenna returned Lita's tremulous smile. "Well, I've always said I'd like to add to my large-animal experience." *And keep my distance from San Jose until I decide what to do with the rest of my life.*

"Trip's office and surgery are over there." Lita pointed to a square clapboard outbuilding across the gravel driveway. "And your rooms are ready for you. I'll show you around after lunch."

Brenna nodded and glanced back at her car. "First, I'd like to get Byron and Malia settled. They're bursting to get out of the car. I hope you don't mind too much that they're with me. Long-term sitters are as hard to find as long-term relief vets during summer vacation."

"Not at all." Lita waved a hand. "With six bedrooms and sixty acres here, Trip has more than enough space. This old house can use the patter of little feet again. I haven't mentioned them to him, but we won't mind a bit."

"I hope not. I brought their kiddie wading pool. As long as they have that and each other, they keep themselves out of trouble."

"They're perfectly welcome," Lita said. "We can both keep an eye on them during the day. I hope they're not allergic to cats, though. I forgot to tell you that Trip has seven calicoes out here. The Dwarves, he calls them. Adopted, of course. I've never known a vet who could resist a homeless animal."

Brenna laughed. "Neither have I, myself included. No, Byron and Malia aren't allergic to anything I know of. Aside from being cooped up in the car for two hours, that is."

"In this heat, who can blame them?" Lita took Brenna's arm. "Lead the way. I'm dying to meet them."

TWO WEEKS FROM THAT DAY, Trip Hart leaned on his crutch in front of the hospital and squinted against the scorching glare of the July sun.

"Home safe," he said into the driver's window of the taxicab. "That's all I ask."

The cabbie looked him over with a dubious eye. "Dispatcher says you'll pay a hundred miles home and a hundred back empty. He's not puttin' me on, is he?"

"You can have your fare up front," Trip assured him.

"You got it, buddy. Hop in . . . I mean, hold on there. I'll give you a hand."

"Stay put." Trip opened the rear door and shoved his aluminum crutch into the back seat.

The driver craned around to give Trip's bandaged head a wary visual examination. Stretching farther, he eyed the full-length plaster cast on Trip's left leg and the one crooking his right arm at a ninety-degree angle. "You *sure* you don't need a hand?"

"Positive. After checking myself out of the hospital against doctor's orders and hiring myself a cab, I'm on a roll." With a grunt, Trip levered himself around on his sound leg.

For an instant during the tricky maneuver, shooting stars seemed to explode between his eyes. Clammy sweat from almost intolerable pain popped out on his forehead and under the elastic bandage bound tight around his bruised ribs. On the verge of passing out, he slid in until his back hit the opposite door and his leg cast lay the length of the back seat. Suppressing a moan, he hooked the end of his crutch in the door handle and yanked it shut.

After assuring that his unusual passenger was wedged safely into the seat, the driver pulled away from the curb.

"Flew the hospital coop, eh?" he commented once they were out of town and on the freeway. "I hate 'em, too. The docs, the shots, the tubes, the whole stinkin' mess. I'd blast out, too. Who wants to spend the biggest holiday of the summer cooped up in a hospital room? Name's Morgan, by the way."

"Hart, here."

"We'll make good time," Morgan observed. "Traffic's light for a Saturday on the Fourth of July weekend. Mind if I smoke?"

"No."

"Join me?"

Trip glanced at the matchbook next to the cigarette pack on the dash and said, "Thanks, but I quit a couple of years ago."

It was a lie, the first of many Trip knew he'd be moved to tell for a while. Until the day he could strike a match like a man again, he'd put a freeze on his pack-a-day vice. Hell, maybe he'd put a freeze on it for good now that he'd gone over two weeks without in the hospital. For years his mother had been nagging him to stop.

He stared at the rigid right angle of his arm and silently cursed his right-handedness. Whether he'd ever be able to do even the simplest thing like a man again remained a dim possibility.

He switched his stony gaze to the passing scenery and mourned the unconscious ease with which he'd formerly lit a cigarette, cut a steak, dealt a round at poker, eased a newborn foal into the world . . . no, he wouldn't think about it. Not today.

"Wish *I* could kick the habit." Morgan sighed as he lit up. "Wife and kids're on my case day and night. When I'm home, that is. 'Hey,' I tell em, 'waitin' around for the next fare's no picnic.' There's a lot of space between fares. With time on my hands and nowhere to go, two packs a day's good company. You married?"

"No." A truth to balance the lie, Trip thought. "Divorced," he volunteered, to escape both craving a smoke and thinking the unthinkable. "My ex had a problem with space, too. There was too much of it for her on my ranch and just what she wanted elsewhere."

Morgan nodded. "I hear ya. I've driven the divorce route, too. But, hey, like they say, it's better the second time around."

"I'm not betting on it." Another solid truth. Even if he *had* been taking odds on it, all bets on any second rounds for himself would be off now. His full lips thinned as grim thoughts crowded in.

After he'd been hurt, his mother had kept reminding him of how lucky he'd been to survive. Neither then nor now did he feel like the good-luck guy. His only luck had been in Lita's being too distraught by his injuries to advance her perpetual one-woman crusade to find her divorced and only son a suitable second wife.

"Don't you *ever* crave a *señorita*?" That had been her favorite inquiry since his divorce, one he'd steadfastly answered with an untruthful and unequivocal negative. His self-imposed and infrequently abandoned celibacy was his own business.

"With that deep red hair and dark eyes, you're the most eligible bachelor in the county," Lita always persisted.

How he had prided himself on the wary distance he kept from women. His involvements had been brief and rare after the divorce, and lately, *date* had become a foreign word to him. He could almost weep at the irony.

Some date he'd be for a woman now, even if he wanted to play that game. Oh, she'd be impressed no end by the dashing figure he cut on a crutch and even more by his sudden inability to make even a simple living at the only profession he knew. The one he loved.

He ground his teeth at that last thought. Tristan Perez Hart, defunct doctor of veterinary medicine. Hell, he wasn't even doctor enough these days to come up with a satisfactory summation of his present condition.

Let's see, paraplegic means two limbs useless. Quadriplegic means all four limbs useless. So there has to be a proper term for left leg and foot at a standstill forever, right arm and hand present but not accounted for. Some interim term such as quasiplegic, *maybe?*

He scowled and switched back to his prior, safer train of thought. That sweet, determined, impossible mother of his. She never gave up. On second thought, she probably *had* spared a moment to spy out a latent wife or two among the several attractive nurses at the hospital.

Think a third time, Trip. Knowing her, she's already hired a live-in nurse to tend you once you're home. She'd consider it a golden opportunity to wave another prospective wife under your nose. Don't forget how she recruited and hired those three "housekeeper/office assistants" she hoped might snag you. The ones you fired as soon as you decently could.

Knowing your mother, she's lined up someone really juicy for your recovery. A blonde with blue eyes, endowed with bodacious everythings, like that one nurse at the hospital.

The hospital nurse had been a blond goddess, nothing short of a centerfold under her starched whites. Even so, his physical and emotional reaction to her and her bodacious endowments had remained purely theoretical. Though she had fluttered her big baby-blues at him when she gave him his daily bath in his bed, it had failed to move him.

Move, shmove. No such luck. For all you know, you're impotent now, as well as crippled.

"You got kids of your own, Hart?"

Trip shifted slightly, painfully in his seat. "One. A daughter. My ex has primary custody."

"Man, my three are all excited about the fireworks and picnics this weekend."

When Trip made no answer, Morgan cleared his throat, turned the radio on, scanned the dial and stopped at a country-western station. "You like country?"

Trip pulled his thoughts back and intercepted the kindly, understanding expression in the driver's eyes. Trust a cab driver who'd seen it all to give space to a man who needed nothing so much as he needed no conversation.

"Sure. Turn it up." Comforted by the driver's easy-going tact, Trip let Willie Nelson's "On the Road Again" drown out the most lethal of his thoughts.

LATER THE SAME DAY, the sun cast long afternoon shadows on the golden hills of the ranch. Inside the century-old ranch house, the countdown had begun.

"...seven, six, five, four, three, two, *one,*" Brenna called out into the staid silence of the parlor. Eyes squeezed shut, she sat beside Lita on an antique horsehair sofa and softly added, "Zero."

Though Malia and Byron never needed more than a slow count of twenty for hide-and-seek, Brenna always extended them that last little bonus. They were both just youngsters after all, whereas she was thirty and Lita sixty. Though they were better at the game than their elders, Brenna couldn't help feeling that age was an unfair advantage.

"Ready or not, *poquitos,* here we come!" Lita warned, and jumped up from the sofa to smooth faded denims over long, slim legs any fashion model would envy. Even after working for two weeks with the older woman, Brenna found herself still struck by the youthful figure Lita maintained with a regimen of yoga and a vegetarian diet. Lita was an independent woman, too, who had restored the Perez family adobe in the village twenty miles away and now lived happily there alone.

Saturday office hours were 10:00 a.m. to 2:00 p.m., and endlessly energetic Lita had stayed late to play what had become a daily game of hide-and-seek with Brenna, Byron and Malia.

By contrast, Brenna struggled only halfway to her feet before flopping back down. "Maybe *you* should go seek while *I* rest these weary bones." She kneaded at a sore muscle in her shoulder. "Birthing a prize baby bull at sunrise this morning did things to this weary vet she can't quite put into words."

Lita nodded. "As the widow of a country vet, *and* the mother of one, I understand completely. But your two little ones won't and you know it."

"You're right. I'd never hear the end of it."

At least, Brenna thought, they had quickly forgiven her for carting them 150 miles from home to the ranch. It was something to be thankful for. Now that she was a self-employed relief veterinarian rather than the full-time clinic vet she had been for the past six years, work and home life had become a real juggling act.

Brenna massaged her other aching shoulder. "Without those two waiting for us to find them, I could curl up here and sleep for hours. The perfect spot for a Saturday afternoon nap."

"Not for napping, *amiga*. Antique horsehair is much too slippery. The only thing it's perfect for is proposals."

Brenna raised her eyebrows in silent inquiry.

"Marriage proposals," Lita explained, her black eyes glowing as she regarded the sofa. "I sat right where you are now when Marcus asked me, on bended knee, to marry him forty-two years ago." She glanced across the room to where framed oil portraits of her late husband and herself, her two daughters and only son hung on the wall above the fieldstone fireplace and added, "I slid right into his arms."

"Oh, gee . . . I had no idea. . . ." Brenna gulped as she rose from her suddenly hot spot.

Lita waved her back. "Sit. It's not a shrine, just special with memories. As I've said before, this old house has a memory around every corner."

She moved to the fireplace and stood smiling at Marcus Hart. "I said yes almost before he got the words out. He was so handsome with that wavy hair. His eyes always surprised me—such a rich, dark brown for a redhead."

Not as dark as Trip's. Brenna focused on the portrait of Trip Hart, Lita's third child and only son. He had his father's wavy hair, a deep red shot through with gold streaks, and his mother's straight, strong Hispanic nose. Each time Trip's image floated vividly to mind as she went about her days, Brenna told herself it wasn't that unnatural to think so often of a man she hadn't even met or spoken to.

In fact, it was quite normal, considering that she, Byron and Malia occupied his house in his absence. After sleeping every night in his house and working his practice for him, she knew more about the man in the portrait than any casual acquaintance would have provided. Given that, thinking about him day and night was no great oddity.

Even so, Brenna felt distinctly uncasual about her ability to mentally summon up every detail of Tristan Perez Hart's likeness on canvas without the slightest effort. She looked away from the portrait now and had no difficulty picturing his square chin, his full lower lip, the red-gold arch of his eyebrows. Yes, the rich brown of his eyes was his father's, but the dark heat in them was all his own.

"Bianca, of course, looks like me," Lita observed. "Elena's an even blend. As for Trip—" she glanced over her shoulder "—what do *you* think, Brenna?"

"Hot." The word licked out like a flame before she could quench it. "That is, he—" she scrambled for balance "—he looks very good with animals. I mean, as if he *is* very good with animals . . ." She only hoped the amber wash of tiny freckles that covered every inch of her tall body would hide the blush that rose to her cheeks.

Lita shot her a look that made Brenna wonder for an instant if yoga induced mind reading. Then, just as quickly, Lita turned back to the portrait.

"Yes, he's wonderful with all creatures, great and small. And sentimental, too. He keeps this old place just as it's always been. Or tries to." She frowned and wiped a fingertip over a dusty hurricane lamp. "I keep telling him he needs someone to help clean more often. And cook, too. He hasn't eaten a decent meal since—well, since before he was married. Suzanne wasn't exactly a gourmet chef." She regarded her dusty finger and then Brenna with a wistful expression. "Maybe after he gets well . . ."

Brenna forced a smile and tried not to think what she knew they were both thinking. The right word was not Lita's hopeful *after*. The word was *if*.

It was ironic that so much had escaped the blaze before it was put out. Except for a blackened corner of the property, the ranch had been spared. At the last minute, the deer had darted away from the oak tree that crashed to earth partly in flames. Trip, though, had been broken by its fall.

It had been Lita who found him and dragged him to safety, badly spraining her wrist in the effort. With her sprain almost healed now, Lita drove a hundred miles every other day to San Luis Obispo where Trip was in the hospital. Her next visit to see him would be tomorrow.

Brenna focused on her hands in her lap. How strange that she should now have cause to hope that Trip Hart's hand, at the very least, would be spared the fate of his paralyzed leg. She who had so recently wished she could trade her own hands for a pair less capable of dashing all her dreams.

Her initial reaction, when her problems began the year before, had been to see her doctor. After being told she was in perfect physical health following an intensive exam, she sought a psychiatric evaluation. The psychiatrist gave her a battery of tests that proved her to be normal.

But that part was now behind her, as was the crushing end of her full-time job. Here at the Hart Ranch was the distance she needed from all that had happened. Here she was finding the space and time to decide what the future held for a seemingly healthy, well-adjusted thirty-year-old who couldn't imagine being anything but a veterinarian.

Doing relief work in San Jose and building up a network of temporary clients while making a decision might have been the smartest thing, but the reminders of what could have been were too numerous, too painful there.

Now Brenna knew she'd made one right decision in heading for the hills. If not for Lita's pleading phone call, she would never have known the pride and satisfaction of delivering a little black bull at sunrise. Nor the joy of playing children's games in this big rambling ranch house with her two loved ones and a woman as special as Trip Hart's mother. Most important, her leaden cloud of pain and loss had lifted just a little, just enough.

Brushing off those troubling thoughts, Brenna stood and hitched up her denim cutoffs. "If I know those two little rascals, they've split up to fake us out. You take the east wing and I'll take the west wing."

"And they'll both get to home base without us." Lita pointed at the horsehair sofa. "As usual, they'll be sitting right there when the game is over—home safe."

Lita and Brenna each carried a dust mop as they headed off in opposite directions to mount their fruitless search. It was one way of holding the inevitable cobwebs and dust balls in the huge house at bay.

Trailing her dust mop during each day's game, Brenna had quickly ferreted out every hiding place in the building. Since she had almost collared Byron in Trip's dark, book-lined study yesterday, she passed that room now and did what she had done every day for two solid weeks. She convinced herself that Trip's bedroom was the likeliest hiding spot today. Byron was probably grinning behind the clothes hanging in Trip's walk-in closet.

"You're in here somewhere, Byron, I can feel it in my bones."

Brenna entered the sunlit bedroom and paused to listen. Not a sound. The blue patchwork quilt and fat down pillows on Trip's carved oak bed were unmussed. His oak nightstand and dresser stood stacked with veterinary journals. A pair of jeans lay draped over a white T-shirt on a willow rocker near the closet.

"I'm moving in on you, little guy."

She tiptoed across the braided rag rug into the dim closet. With her mop handle she gently prodded behind the clothes on hangers. No Byron. As usual. She was alone, as she had known she would be, surrounded by the scent of wool, tobacco, boot leather, the combined scent of a man she had come to know more intimately than might be best.

Not for the first time in her fortnight at the ranch, Brenna leaned on her mop in his closet, closed her eyes and breathed deep of Trip Hart's masculine essence. It held no hint of after-shave or cologne, just as his closet held no dress clothes or formal shoes that she could see without snooping, and she was no snoop. It left her to wonder what he wore when he went out with a woman. Old corduroys and one of those fisherman knit sweaters on the overhead shelf? The T-shirt and pair of jeans draped on the rocker?

Not for the first time in her closet musings, Brenna considered what those last two items implied of their wearer. His jeans' waist and length proved he was slim hipped and taller than her five feet ten inches. His wide leather belt was still looped in his jeans, indicating that he was a man of no wasted motion.

She rested her chin on the mop handle. Dear heaven. She could imagine him coming out of those clothes in two quick moves. How would a man like that come to terms with a disabled arm and leg? For such a man, every physical move hereafter would be frustration, humiliation, agony.

Unable to stand the thought of it, Brenna replaced that distressing image with one of Trip as he might look after his two quick moves and before the accident. She pictured him uninjured, strong, virile. In her mind she visualized crisp hair massed on his broad chest and at his groin, hair a darker gold-shot red than that on his head.

With a silky inner shiver she turned her thoughts from the burnished splendor of his nude body to his bed. Had it, as Lita once remarked obliquely, been as cold in the years after his divorce as Brenna's still remained after hers? Did that account for the dark, slow burn in his eyes?

No stranger to sidelined passions herself, she wondered how Trip dealt with his if what Lita implied was true. One-night stands? He didn't seem the type, though a man with his looks wouldn't have any trouble lining up as many as he wanted.

What sort of husband, lover, had he been? After a few moments' speculation on the possibilities that provocative question summoned up, Brenna shook herself back to reality and brushed aside the erotic fantasies her vivid imagination seemed always eager to paint where Trip was concerned.

She hadn't even met this man who lay miles away in a hospital with debilitating injuries, yet here she lingered, thinking long and hard about him standing stark naked in his bedroom. Idiot.

2

BRENNA HUSTLED OUT of Trip's closet with her dust mop and started working up a sweat over the dust under his big oak bed. Fantasize about something besides him warming it up with you, she chided herself as she dusted. And get those jeans on the rocker out of your rocker. He won't be shucking those off in one fast move for a long time, if ever. Don't forget that.

Outside on the front porch, Trip sweated bullets as he sagged against the battered screen door and signaled Morgan to move on. He squinted down the long gravel driveway and watched the yellow taxi roll away. Who would have thought his own driveway would one day count as the longest journey of his life?

Morgan hadn't liked the idea of letting his ailing passenger off at the gate but had cowed under Trip's adamant gaze. Trip hadn't let on that he was covering up cowardice with what only looked like courage. He hadn't expected his mother's car to be parked in the driveway. She always left early on Saturdays and spent the afternoon at his sister's place an hour's drive away.

If he was lucky, she was now stuffing the relief vet's face with an early supper in the kitchen at the rear of the house. He hoped so. He had to somehow sneak in without her knowing he'd arrived. She could cuss in Spanish so long and loud a man's ears would ring for hours afterward.

His ears were already ringing from either the drugs he'd been force-fed in the hospital or the blow to his head. He wasn't sure which. Paired with the constant pain of just breathing, it was clamor enough to push anyone beyond the boundaries of civility and patience. He hadn't demonstrated either virtue this morning at the hospital as he checked himself out. His doctor had been spitting mad but helpless. Trip knew the feeling all too well.

With painful stealth, he eased the front door open and hobbled in. He shuffled through the foyer and paused to groan softly in the parlor as shooting stars exploded again behind his closed eyelids. Only a few more steps.

He had taken just one when, below the high-pitched whine in his ears, he heard a muffled sound behind him. He looked around. Nothing there. Take it easy, he told himself. He'd been riddled with so many hypodermics for the past two weeks it was little wonder he'd begun hearing sounds, as well as seeing stars.

It was when he faced forward to take another torturous step that he saw the woman across the room. She was backing through the doorway between the parlor and the hall swiping a dust mop at the ceiling and muttering to herself.

Was she real or a hallucination? He squinted beyond the shooting stars. Real. Yes, he'd fired enough of Lita's hirelings to recognize this as yet another. This one had slim, tanned legs that even a half-delirious man could see were made to wear the denim cutoffs slung low on her hips. What of it, though? He scowled. What could he do about a great pair of legs now even if he wanted to? Nothing.

That, added to the fact that she was wearing one of the blue scrub shirts he did surgery in, was suddenly too damned much. The compressed fury of his pain exploded into words.

"When did she hire *you*?" he spat out.

She whirled around and met his unsteady stare with eyes the precise color of the Spanish cream sherry he kept stocked in the cellar. In contrast to the pale brown of her straight hair and the paler spray of freckles on her fair skin, her brows and lashes looked almost black. Or was he seeing things?

"I started two weeks ago," she replied with what appeared to be a major effort. Through the storm of shooting stars, Trip now confirmed that the rich amber of her shocked gaze was no mirage. She was quite beautiful.

Infuriated even further by that fact, which should have remained irrelevant, he hobbled forward a step and swayed on his crutch at a fresh wave of pain so intense it impelled him to pose his next question through gritted teeth.

"What are you doing?"

"I'm—" she jiggled the mop "—dusting." Her dark, winged eyebrows drew into a slight frown as if in wonder at the question.

"Dusting. I get it. My mother the matchmaker strikes again with another housekeeper. What's she up to here? Besides setting you up for two weeks' notice, that is."

She cupped her hands over the top of the mop handle and said, "We're both playing hide-and-seek at the moment, but—"

"No buts, please." He passed a trembling hand over his clammy brow. "Hide-and-seek with a dust mop?"

"Yes. You see, whenever we play hide-and—"

"On second thought, skip the explaining. It could only make sense to my mom the yoga freak and someone else on the same crazy wavelength. It beats staring at your navel, I guess. Who's 'it'? You, Mom or the dust mop?"

She surprised him with a flash of indignation in her lovely eyes as she replied, "This mop and I have been dusting *your* house for you. It's Byron and Malia who are 'it.'"

"Byron and who?"

"Malia. They're mine."

Now he felt truly spent, goaded beyond his last shred of civility or patience for his mother or anyone else. "Kids?" he growled, blearily shaking his head. "You have two kids? She must be getting desperate."

Even as pain threatened his self-control, Trip had to admire the woman's dignity as she drew herself up to her considerable height and countered, "They're not my kids."

"Not yours?" He stared at her in arch disbelief. "Whose are they? Or have I finally lucked out with a housekeeper who's happily married?"

"I'm divorced. They're adopted."

Instantly he regretted rolling his eyes. They felt like ground glass in their sockets, spurring him to sneer, "Great. Adopted. Bighearted of you."

"Not at all. They needed a loving home. I had one to offer."

"Charitable of you, then. So *that's* your specialty. Wouldn't you know she'd find a bleeding heart." He let out a grating sigh. "Just what I need around here. Trust my matchmaking mother to hire the perfect mate for Trip the Crip."

"She didn't hire me for that," Brenna retorted, frowning.

"That's what you think. You don't know my mother like I do." He ground his teeth at both his physical agony and the phantom noises that had returned to undercut the ringing in his ears. "Take my advice, miss. Pack your bags and save your charity."

"I'm not offering it. I—"

"Save it," he broke in. "My mother made a mistake. I don't need a housekeeper. And if she hinted that I'm in the market for a *señorita*, don't take the hint, *señorita*. I'm one nasty man who doesn't want a clean house, or a housekeeper with kids, or anyone else in my life right now."

Brenna stood even taller. "You're in luck on the first two counts at the moment, *señor*."

"Inform my mother of it, would you? And remind her that my one and only rug rat is the only child I want to support." He glanced past Brenna's shoulder into the hall. "When do *your* rug rats come out of the woodwork?"

"They're already out and home safe." She pointed at the horsehair sofa behind him.

Trip pivoted on his crutch and stared, appalled. Two weeks of doctors and drugs had finally triumphed. Not only was he hearing things, he was seeing more than stars.

From their seat on the sofa, the two tiniest, daintiest, blackest little pigs in kingdom come grunted and grinned sweetly up at him.

"Pygmalia and Lard Byron," Brenna commanded, "say hello to the master of the house."

Before they could obey, Trip collapsed to the floor.

"OH, *POBRECITO*," Lita whimpered ten minutes later when she and Brenna won their superwoman struggle to slide a limp, unconscious Trip onto his bed.

Lita plucked at the perspiration-soaked red sport shirt he wore. "What is he doing out of the hospital? Dr. Jamison said another week at the very least."

Brenna measured his pulse and murmured, "I'd have prescribed longer, myself." She looked up from her wristwatch. "He's okay for the moment. His respiration and pulse are normal."

"But he's so pale, *amiga* . . . and look how they cut off the leg of the new pants I bought for him to wear home when he . . . oh, why did he . . . *how* did he get home?"

Brenna shook her head. "I don't know. I turned around and poof! There he was. How are *you* doing, by the way? How's your wrist?"

"Worse...but what does that matter when Trip is...is he going to be all right? *Madre Maria*, if he—"

"He'll be fine," Brenna assured her, convinced by Trip's strong vital signs that it was true for the moment. "Hold your arm up so the blood runs the other way, Lita."

Lita hiked her arm overhead and moved to where Byron and Malia stood in the doorway and watched like the polite Chinese Potbelly Miniature pet pigs they were.

"Shall I call 911, Brenna?"

Brenna lifted Trip's eyelids. "His pupils aren't dilated. Breathing's normal. Maybe you should get his doctor on the phone first. And round up a pair of sharp scissors before you do."

"Whatever you say. *Ay, Chihuahua.* I'm so glad there's a doctor in the house."

She scurried out with Brenna's pet pigs dogging her heels, while Brenna wet a washcloth and grabbed a towel out of the bathroom adjacent to Trip's closet.

Lita rushed back with the scissors. "I'll call Dr. Jamison," she promised as she headed out again. "The number's in the kitchen."

"Good. Yell down the hall when you get him on the line, and I'll pick up the extension in here."

Lita held her swollen wrist high as she reached the door and then stopped. "*Amiga*...what are the scissors for?"

"Nothing gory. He's perspired all the way through his clothes. They'll have to be cut off. He could get chilled, which wouldn't be good." Brenna glanced from Lita's wrist to Trip's arm cast. "Since I'm the only one with two good hands around here, I'll do it."

"Do whatever you have to, *muchacha*. Are you sure he's okay otherwise?"

"Positive. Go call the doctor. Oh, and put Byron and Malia in their pen if you get a chance. We don't need them underfoot."

"*Sí*. Come, *pollitos*."

Brenna saw the excited light in her pet pigs' eyes die and mentally berated herself for not spelling out the word *pen* as she usually did. She even suspected they'd picked up some Spanish from Lita. She sighed and endured the guilt of hearing eight tiny, dejected hooves trail Lita down the hall. Oh, well. They'd get over it by supper time.

She turned back to Trip and held a hand to his cheek. Warmth and color were returning to his clammy skin. His breathing was deep and rhythmic. He was fast asleep.

She slid a pillow under his head, then examined the household shears with a surgeon's scrutiny. Shirt first or pants? Before Brenna could decide which to cut into, though, Lita came skidding back through the door. The pigs, bright eyed at their sudden reprieve, were right on her heels.

"The phone in the kitchen's dead!"

Brenna picked up the extension on Trip's night table. "Dead here, too. The lines must be down somewhere again."

Huge tears brimmed in Lita's dark eyes as she cradled her sprained wrist in the opposite hand. "Now what?"

Now what? Brenna drew a shaky breath. "One thing that's got to hit the ice is your arm, Lita. It's swelling like a balloon."

"But Trip—what about *him*?"

"Don't worry. Horses, dogs and men are all mammals. As a vet, I'm not that different from an M.D." She said it more to reassure both herself and Lita than as a statement of absolute fact. "You tend to that wrist. I'll tend to Trip."

"But he—"

"Fill the kitchen sink with ice and water and stick your arm in. Hurry up before it gets worse. Soak it for at least fifteen minutes. Where's that elastic bandage you wore last week?"

"I don't know. Somewhere around."

"Find it. I'll bind your wrist and rig up a sling when I'm through here." When Lita still hesitated, Brenna prodded, "Go on. You can't nurse Trip with one hand."

"I know. If only my wrist wasn't so weak, I'd..." Lita's frown lessened a fraction as she turned to leave. "I'm so lucky you're here, Brenna. First the *poquitos* to the *p-e-n*, then the ice. I'll find the bandage. *Gracias, amiga*."

Brenna turned back to Trip and flexed the scissors in her hand. She was glad Lita wasn't present to watch his red sport shirt take the first cut. It looked as new as the khaki twill pants with the left leg cut off for Trip's cast. Still it had to be cut. There was no way to maneuver the garment off with him lying on his back. She started cutting.

As she pulled the scraps of his shirt from around and under him, she reflected that undressing a sick, sleeping man with scissors was a lot simpler than the tedious shaving of fur a sick dog or cat could require before surgery. Focusing on that kept her from marveling too much at how precisely the red-gold hair on Trip's broad chest matched the mental image she had so often conjured up.

Really, Brenna. Aren't his casts and bandages a solemn enough sight? This is no time for flights of fancy.

As she unbuckled his belt and slid it through its loops, she had to sternly remind herself that Trip deserved as much professionalism as she would want her own physician to exercise. Would she want a doctor or nurse thinking anything other than clinical thoughts as her clothing was peeled off her body? Never.

With that firmly in mind, she cut Trip's clammy pants off him and put his wallet and change on the dresser. Then she turned to the final matter of his underwear.

He's just a man, Brenna, no different from your former husband and the two losers you wasted yourself on right after the divorce.

But as she snipped his briefs to ribbons, it became frankly apparent that he was every bit the man she had so often imagined—and then some.

Feeling at once light-headed and entirely unprofessional over that quite unscientific observation, she sponged Trip down with the washcloth and toweled him dry. By the time she finally drew the patchwork quilt over him, she felt as if she could use a sponge bath herself. Thank heaven, she wasn't his personal physician. She'd have had to resign the case. Even bound up in bandages and casts, his was not a physique an observant red-blooded woman could easily ignore.

As Brenna debated whether to tend to Lita or stay with Trip, he stirred. A moaning sound escaped his lips as he clawed the air with his good hand. Brenna caught his hand in hers and sat on the edge of the bed.

"Shh. It's okay. You're okay," she soothed. He seemed more sick child than primal male now, whimpering, incoherent, his hand gripping hers for dear life.

"Water . . ."

She rushed to the bathroom and back.

"Here." Propping his head up, she held the glass to his lips. Eyes closed, he gulped greedily, noisily before sinking back onto the pillow.

"Thanks, Mom. . . ." His fingers tugged at the gauze bandage around his head.

"No, no," Brenna protested in a soft whisper. "Don't do that. Hush, now." She wrapped her fingers around his hand and restrained it in her lap as he quieted. What head wound did that bandage conceal? Now she wished Lita had gone into greater detail about his multiple injuries.

Damn the phone lines that seemed to go down with the slightest breeze in these hills! This was twice now in the same week that phone service had been interrupted. The last time it had taken eight hours until the line was repaired. No wonder no call had come from the hospital to warn that Trip was on his way.

Brenna stroked his hand and glanced down as it slowly relaxed open in her lap. It was warm and heavy against her bare legs. His fingers were strong and well shaped, his thumb long and determined, his palm square. Without consciously intending it, she gently straightened the inward curve of his fingers and focused in on what the pattern of lines on his palm told of their owner.

His heart line was etched deep and parted in a small fork on the round pad of flesh under his index finger. So he was an idealist, she thought, one whose heart had been broken, according to a long falling branch from the line.

His head line, long and slightly curved, revealed a practical mind-set, intelligent and even. His line of life was deep and arched around the base of his thumb in a wide, sweeping curve.

She felt her cheeks warm as she studied that generous, life-embracing curve. Idealistic, yet endowed with the sensual passions of a realist. A man with a life line like this rarely did anything halfway personally or professionally. As for his two marriage lines—

"Were those pigs real?"

She gasped. Her head shot up. The deadpan question had come from Trip. Eyes wide open, he was looking straight at her.

"Were they?" His second inquiry was made in the same steely, steady tone as the first, accompanied by the same inscrutable, opaque gaze.

"Yes. They're Chinese Potbelly Miniatures. I . . ." She looked down at his hand in hers and dropped it with guilty haste as she bolted to her feet.

"Second question. Were you reading my palm?"

"I . . . you were . . . tearing at your bandage . . . on your head . . . and, well, I held your hand . . . so you wouldn't . . . ."

Good heavens, when had he come back from dreamland? How long had she been decoding the secrets of his palm? He looked as if he'd been awake for hours, staring at her like that.

"Were you?" he inquired in the same even tone. "Or weren't you?"

"Well, I . . ." Brenna squared her shoulders, "I was reading it, yes. A harmless hobby I picked up from my grandmother."

"And what great good fortune awaits me?"

His voice remained a cool monotone, but the icy expression in his eyes had warmed to resemble the dark heat that fired his portrait on the parlor wall. Not a cozy warmth at the moment, Brenna decided.

Her only comfort lay in the fact that she towered over him even as he intimidated her with his burning stare. Don't let him, she told herself.

"What's the prognosis?" he persisted, as the flame in his eyes heated to an angry blaze.

"Excellent. It appears you've survived your fainting spell without lessening your foul mood and temper one little bit," she replied.

"Fainting spell," he snorted. "I didn't faint. I've had a rotten day. I passed out."

"And *I* hauled you off the floor and into bed. I was just holding your hand so you wouldn't rip your hat off."

"You put me in bed?"

She nodded. "Lita helped."

"That still doesn't give you any right." He held up his hand, palm outward, in an accusing gesture. "You invaded my privacy."

"Only if you believe the lines mean something."

"Leave the psychic mumbo jumbo to my ex-wife. I don't buy any of it." He shoved his hand under the covers at his chest. "You trespassed on private property just the same, though."

"I did that before I looked at your palm." Now that his blood had returned to a rolling boil, he might as well know the worst. Brenna sent a meaningful glance down the length of the patchwork quilt.

His eyes went from smoldering to stricken as he shrank down under his cover. "I thought Mom . . . you mean *you* . . . stripped my . . . ?"

"Yes, Dr. Hart. Down to the bare essentials." To cover her sudden blush, she gathered up her scissors and the rags that had been his clothes and made a smoke screen bustle of setting them aside. "Sorry about that, but it had to be done. A chill is the last thing you need in your condition."

"You sound more like a nurse than a housekeeper."

"Try relief vet."

He opened his mouth and closed it, blinked and then stared at her. "What did you say?"

"I'm Brenna Deveney." She frowned at him, perplexed, fearing suddenly that he might be suffering some sort of amnesia from his fall.

"Relief vet," he repeated, realization coming to a slow dawn in his eyes.

"The vet Lita hired," Brenna prompted. "Remember?"

"Brenna J. Deveney?"

"Yes. The J stands for Jeanne."

Trip wiped his hand over his eyes and looked daunted for the first time since he'd opened them. Good God. So that's what Lita had been cooking up in his absence. Deveney. The relief vet. "Where is she?"

"I'm right here."

"Not you. My mother. Where?"

"Packed in ice up to her elbow in the kitchen sink. She sprained her wrist again helping me drag you into bed."

"Oh." He chewed the inside of his lower lip for a moment and considered Brenna with a wary eye. "Is she, um, all right otherwise?"

"Yes. She's fine, except for the wrist." Brenna did a double take as his expression at her reply went suddenly apprehensive, almost sheepish.

"Good. She's fine." Eyes up, he considered the ceiling, thinking. "When does she come out of the sink?"

"Soon. Shall I get her for you?"

"Not yet." He patted the edge of the mattress. "Have a seat. So. You're my relief vet. How are things going?"

"Busy." She perched warily on the spot he'd patted. "Today was slow, though."

He nodded. "It always is during the Fourth. Well. You've gotten to know Mom fairly well since you came?"

"More than fairly, I'd say."

"Excitable, isn't she? Except when she's tied up in yoga knots and contemplating her navel or her karma, I mean."

"Excitable? I don't know if I'd . . ."

"Look, you don't have to be polite. I mean, she's my mother and all, but we both know how intense she can get at times."

"Well, intense was one word for her reaction when she walked in and saw that you'd fai—er, passed out." Brenna shrugged. "It didn't help that you were chalk white and flat on your back."

"What did she do?"

"What any mother would do. She burst into tears."

"Did she cry in Spanish?"

When he flinched slightly as he posed that question, Brenna knew that she positively had his number. It would come in handy, too. That psychological screw could be twisted to a certain advantage when he got grim and gritty again. Based on the past half hour, that promised to be any minute now.

"'Cry in Spanish?'" she repeated blankly. There was no law against playing dumb until an opportunity to twist came along.

"Never mind," he snapped. He drummed the fingers of his good hand on his upper chest. "Forget it."

"All right. How are you feeling, by the way?"

"Take a wild guess." His face darkened again. "Now that you've had a good long look at my marriage lines and a longer one at the family jewels, how do *you* think I feel? Try exposed, for a start."

"Appreciative would be more appropriate. I could have let you lie here and catch pneumonia." Brenna stood up and glowered back at him. "With a disposition like yours, I'm surprised they didn't kick you out of the hospital a week ago."

"No one kicked me out of anything. I kicked myself out. I won my freedom on my own."

"Then why don't you lie back and enjoy it?" She walked to the door and paused there to administer the first well-deserved twist. "Excuse me, but I have a sprained wrist to attend to."

"Wait! Don't leave!" He shot upward from the shoulders and then sank back with a strangled groan as the binding around his ribs arrested the movement.

"Relax. I'm only going to tell Lita you're awake. I'll be back."

"No! Don't do that!"

"Okay. I *won't* be back. I'll return to enjoying the nice day it was before you limped in the front door."

"No, no. I meant, don't tell her I'm awake."

"Why not?"

"Because I said so. Isn't that reason enough? Cripes. Give a man a break. I swear, she hires nothing but morons around here, whether they're housekeepers or relief vets. Does everything have to be spelled out for you word for word?"

Now he was really asking for it, and more than ever he deserved it. "I've never won a spelling bee," she retorted, "but I do know that Lita's worried sick. Why don't you want her to know you're back in the land of the living?"

He expelled a harsh, impatient sigh. "Use your head for something more than cutting a man's clothes into confetti for a closer look, would you?"

"Why you—why don't *you* just spit out whatever's stuck in your throat. Maybe I read your palm when you weren't looking, but I can't read your mind."

"Thank fate for small favors," he growled. "It may be the only private part I've got left now that you've stripped me bare otherwise."

She took a step through the door. "I'll get Lita for you."

"Just tell her I'm still asleep."

"Has anyone ever advised you that a please or a thank-you can go a long way toward getting you what you want?"

He puffed out his cheeks in a testy sigh. "Don't make things any worse than they are. I'm not in the mood. My head is killing me and so is my arm. Just tell her."

"Sorry, Doctor. I never lie if I don't have to."

"I suppose you don't follow orders with good grace, either," he groused. "Some relief vet I end up with."

"Some boss *I* end up with," she rejoined. "Now I see why you've never hired an associate vet even though your practice appears to need one. Who would work for you?"

"I'll worry about my own business affairs, if you don't mind. I'm the employer here."

"The *former* employer," Brenna corrected, "unless you stop ordering me around like your slave. I don't work for doctors who can't spare proper respect or consideration for their employees."

"You're a professional. You can't just walk out without giving notice," Trip said with a dark scowl. "If you do, you'll never get a glowing reference from me, Dr. Deveney."

"I'm not sure I want one from you, Dr. Hart." She was glad to see he looked ready to pop at that. "Anything I can get for you while I'm gone? Something to rip and tear at besides me? A cigarette to huff and puff on, perhaps? There's a carton of stale ones in the kitchen."

"I quit smoking in the hospital."

"Lita will be thrilled to hear it. She'll be in to see you in just a moment."

He glared at her, a man twisted finally into blurting, "What do you want me to do? Beg? Can't you see she'll eat me alive for dinner if she gets me alone?"

"In that case, I'll say you're awake, the minute she asks. And then I'll say—" Brenna gave him her sweetest smile with the final twist "—*bon appétit*."

3

"HE'S AWAKE."

Lita jerked her lower arm out of the sink at the news and pivoted around on her kitchen stool. The wooden perch tottered under her. Ice water dripped from her arm onto the thighs of her jeans as she made the sign of the cross with her swollen hand three times in a row.

"*Gracias, Madre Maria.* How is he?"

"Fine. Scratching and biting like a sick bobcat, but cowering under the covers like a whipped pup whenever your name comes up."

Lita heaved a big sigh of relief. "That sounds like Trip when he's been bad." She slipped off the stool and reached for a towel. "Just wait till I sink my teeth into him. Out of the hospital a week early. Scaring me to death." She dried her wet arm vigorously with the towel, "*Caramba*, does he have some explaining to do."

"Lita, easy on that wrist. Here, sit back down. Where's your bandage?"

Lita grabbed the long elastic strip off the counter and thrust it at Brenna. "Hurry, *amiga*. I have fish to fry with that son of mine."

"Hold still." Brenna began wrapping Lita's wrist, then paused to glance up. Lita looked ferocious. Perhaps Trip deserved a break, after all. "He's hurting pretty bad, you know. Don't be too hard on him if you can help it."

"He'll hurt a lot worse when I get through with him." Lita's eyes flashed anger even as they glistened with tears.

"After all I've done for that *hombre*—driving back and forth to the hospital—holding down the fort—hiring you to keep his practice going—"

"Speaking of me, Lita, he mistook me for a house-keeper until I set him straight a minute ago."

Lita gulped and looked taken aback, then sheepish. "Oh, dear. He knows you're the vet?"

"Yes."

Lita crossed herself again and rolled her eyes beseech-ingly heavenward.

"What's wrong?"

"There's something I haven't told you, *amiga*," Lita said, tucking a strand of hair back into her braid. "You see, I hate to think of him out here alone, without a woman and children to love. I've been trying to match him up with someone ever since Suzanne ran off. He lost all patience with me a few months ago, and flew off the handle. We had words and didn't speak for a week."

Brenna fastened the bandage tight and stood back to frown at her patient. "So?"

Lita swallowed hard. "I didn't tell him I hired a woman. I didn't want another fight over matchmaking. I thought I'd wait until he felt better. I was going to break it to him gently next week before he came home."

Brenna stared at her as several things clicked into place in her head. "That's why he got so angry thinking I was a housekeeper."

"*Sí*. It's my fault. This place has been a revolving door when it comes to housekeepers and office assistants." She twisted a button on her chambray shirt with her good hand and fixed Brenna with a dark, entreating gaze. "What else could I do? I tried to get a man out here. You were the only relief vet who could come out of the ten I called. That's why I told him only most of the truth. You don't know Trip when his blood is up. He'd never have gotten a wink of sleep in the hospital. He'd have accused me of matchmaking. I wasn't. I've learned my lesson. No more housekeepers. *Ay, Chihuahua.* As fast as I hired them, he fired them."

Brenna wilted and leaned against the kitchen counter for support. "What exactly did you say when you told him about me?"

"I told him I hired a young relief vet, B. J. Deveney, from San Jose. 'B.J.'s doing a fine job,' I said whenever he asked in the hospital. 'B.J.'s just great. No problem.'" She crossed herself again and added, "It was the truth. I would never tell an outright lie to Trip or anyone else."

"Tell that to Trip. Now I know why he looked ready to explode when he found out who I was." Brenna pushed away from the counter. "You'd better get in there and make a clean breast of it, Lita. Right away. I'll pack and go if he insists on having a man out here, but I'd rather stay if I can. I need the work."

"Yes, of course I'll tell him everything."

"Good. That's one problem solved." But as Brenna knotted a clean cotton towel into a sling, she could see that Lita looked as edgy about facing Trip as Trip had looked about telling his mother he'd dropped in a week early. Lita's arm felt rigid with anxiety as Brenna arranged it in the sling.

"There." She tightened the knot on the towel and headed for the back door. "Go and get it over with."

"Aren't you coming with me?"

"Into a room with a man ready to blow sky-high? I've been bloodied enough for one day, thank you."

"Where are you going?"

"Outside to feed Byron and Malia."

"*Ave Maria.* Trip's going to roast me for dinner when he sees me. His own mother."

Brenna concealed a wry smile as she left Lita to her Hail Marys. *Bon appétit, Trip.*

THE ERUPTION of two volatile voices in Spanish suited Independence Day weekend to a tee. Across the driveway from the house, Brenna leaned against the cyclone fence of the dog run that now doubled as a pigpen and watched her loved ones enjoy their Sunday supper. Three of Trip's seven cats rubbed around her calves. The only conflicting notes in the peaceful scene were the Hispanic fireworks exploding through Trip's open bedroom window. Mother and son were certainly making this Brenna's most memorable Fourth.

She decided there was no reason to cover her ears, even though she was one of the issues. Spanish was a foreign tongue to her, though anyone could deduce from the decibel level and tone of Trip's voice that whatever he had to say about his mother's deception would have scorched Brenna's ears.

Even Byron and Malia looked up from their absorption in supper at one particularly voluble exchange. Their bright-eyed gazes met Brenna's as the debate rose to a crescendo and ceased with the loud slam of an inner door. Next came the slam of the back door. Then came Lita fuming around the corner of the house, headed straight for her car. Her left arm was out of the sling, but the bandage was still intact.

Brenna reached her just as the car door slammed shut. "What happened?" She bent to peer in at Lita.

"He can take care of himself, if that's the way he wants to be about it!" Lita's cheeks flamed and her eyes sparked as she started the engine and lapsed into an indignant rapid-fire stream of Spanish.

"You told him?"

"*Sí, muchacha.* He knows everything. And so do I. Against the doctor's orders—coming home in a taxi! He's *loco.* I'm through with him. *Macho. Loco. No-no.* And I am not a matchmaker, whatever he wants to think." She threw the automatic into reverse.

Brenna grabbed the door handle. "Whoa there. What am I supposed to do now? Pack my bags or stay?"

"He agreed you would stay when I agreed not to call an ambulance to take him back to the hospital. Now, let him stew in his own juice. If he got his broken bones out of the hospital, he can decide what to do with them for the rest of the day."

"But, Lita, somebody's got to give him a hand here. He can barely move even with a crutch."

Lita shook her head vehemently and revved the engine. "He can figure that out for himself. He's thirty-five years old. A grown man. I am not my son's keeper. Let him stew. I'll see you on Tuesday."

"What about the rest of the weekend?"

"Monday is Independence Day. I'm declaring my independence two days early. *Adios, amiga.*"

Helpless to stop her, Brenna watched the white sedan speed out the gravel driveway. Across the driveway, Byron and Malia pricked their ears forward and kicked at the fence of their kennel to get out. When she didn't move for several moments, they both grunted softly at her and kicked harder.

She turned to meet their eager, inquiring eyes. "Don't look at me like that. I'm not his keeper, either."

S<small>OME VIEW</small>. Trip stared up at the cracks in the plaster ceiling. One heck of a view. He craned his head sideways on the pillow, slowly, slowly so the pounding and ringing wouldn't start up again.

Through the screen of his open window he saw Brenna standing in the middle of his driveway with her hands on her hips, choking on the exhaust of his mother's departure. Beyond her, across the wide driveway, his earlier hallucinations nosed the fence of the dog run.

So this is B. J. Deveney, D.V.M. Surprise! B.J., Pygmalia and Lard Byron, one happy little family.

As he watched, Brenna scowled and kicked a spray of gravel into the air with a sneakered foot. Three of the Dwarves went scrambling for cover as her lips moved in what was clearly no expression of glee.

Serves her right for turning Lita loose on a broken, helpless man. She brought it on herself.

He saw her take a step forward and squint down the driveway, as if hoping Lita might make a U-turn. Her hope apparently didn't materialize for she shifted her squint to the sun, fanned the front of his oversize green surgery shirt against her chest and then impatiently stripped it off like a T-shirt.

Trip's eyes widened as the garment cleared her head to reveal the skimpy yellow tube top she wore. Not a man to ignore one heck of a view, he levered painfully up on his good elbow for a better look. She shook her shiny hair out, tucked the sides behind her ears and just stood there, scowling.

Tall and slender in her short denim cutoffs, with every rich curve of her full, firm breasts outlined in golden relief by the setting sun, she filled his eyes as he couldn't remember any woman doing in recent history. Not even the hospital nurse with the centerfold proportions had looked quite this—well, outright sexy.

Trip's gaze roved down to her long, shapely legs, and he remembered how he had floated back to consciousness an hour earlier with his hand cradled between her smooth, bare thighs. How long had he lain there then, a silent captive of her touch? It had seemed like forever.

Something—a strange, ethereal energy—had seemed to flow through him from her as she examined his hand, a stream of soothing balm that halved his pain even as her touch and closeness doubled a surge of unexpected physical desire. Or had he imagined it, just as he had imagined making love to her? How long had he studied her lightly freckled face and thighs, all the while willing his hot, hard erection to subside as she studied his palm? Only when mind had triumphed over matter had he broken silence.

Now, as he remembered her spirited response when he finally had spoken, his groin throbbed for a second time since his accident. She had been a real beauty, defying him with her quick tongue and those flashing amber eyes.

Twice now, and both in the space of an hour. And each time B. J. Deveney brought you to life.

Yes, her hardheaded refusal to give an inch in the face of his growls and snarls had been a show to watch. Then and now, she was gorgeous.

It almost hurt when she moved out of the frame of his bedroom window. He was left to ease gingerly back to his pillow and contemplate the afterglow of her sun-splashed image in his mind. He slid his good hand down to confirm, with a mixture of regret and relief, the hard evidence that sexually, at least, he remained what he had once been. It wasn't a lot for a man with a useless arm and leg to give thanks for, but it was better than nothing at all.

"WHERE'S MY CRUTCH!"

Two doors from Trip's room, Brenna's head snapped up from her pillow. She blinked away a lingering fragment of a fitful dream. But for a silvery square of moonlight on her bed, her room was dark.

She sat up and clutched her comforter to the semi-sheer cotton batiste of her white, frilled nightshirt. Where *was* Trip's crutch? Or had she merely dreamed that bellowed question?

Twice before retiring for the evening, she had knocked softly and tiptoed into Trip's room. His motionless form under the quilt and his light snore had told her he was asleep both times. After the eleven-o'clock news there had been little to do but put the Dwarves out and tuck the pigs safely away in the infirmary. With the phone lines still down, Trip's doctor couldn't be called. So Brenna had gone to bed with her fingers crossed. After a Saturday unlike any she'd spent in her life, sleep had descended on her like a tidal wave.

"Where's my crutch!" The repeated demand was punctuated by an even louder thump and the crash of breaking glass.

Brenna leaped out of bed. The bellowing bull in the china shop was no nightmare. He was Trip Hart. She struggled into a short batiste robe that matched her short nightshirt. Maybe firecracker Lita could refuse to be her adult son's keeper, but Brenna was a licensed doctor of animal medicine with a professional code to uphold when it came to all living things. Dog, cat or Trip Hart, she couldn't turn her back on an animal in distress.

Careening down the hall, she cringed at a second loud crash, one she hoped hadn't rendered him unconscious again.

Into his moonlit room she rushed and flipped the overhead light on. A Tiffany lamp and his water glass lay smashed on the floor. Nude except for his casts and bandages, Trip half sprawled, half sat on the edge of the bed.

He blinked in the sudden burst of light and snatched the quilt across his hips when he saw her. She felt her face contort with pain in an empathetic imitation of his at the agony the abrupt movement had caused him.

"My crutch," he demanded between gritted teeth. "I need it. Hurry."

Eyes wide, she scanned the room. No crutch. She turned and ran out to the parlor, snapping lights on as she went. The events of the afternoon and evening whirled through her mind as her eyes darted around the room. Good grief, where was it?

There! Under the horsehair sofa where Lita had kicked it out of the way after Trip had fallen. Brenna raced back with it and helped Trip slide over to the opposite side of the bed to avoid the broken glass. That accomplished, she held his crutch steady for him as he strained to both rise and retain his modesty at the same time.

"Here, Trip. Lean on me. No, not like that. Slide over. Put your hand right here on the crutch." Panting with her own efforts as her patient swallowed audible groans, she struggled to maneuver both man and crutch upright and failed miserably.

Within the space of a few daunting seconds, she had to straighten up and say, "You'll have to drop the fig leaf. You need that hand on the crutch if you want to stand up."

If anything, he clutched the quilt closer while still struggling to come upright.

She puffed out an impatient breath. "Where are you going in such a hurry?"

He yanked his head toward the bathroom. "Where do you think?"

"Here, lie back down and I'll try to get these on you." Brenna reached out to the rocking chair and snatched up the jeans that had resided there since before his accident.

"Won't work," he muttered.

"Drop the modesty, then. I don't have a spare bedpan lying around right now." At the pained look on his face as he hesitated, she added, "Look, I've worked in a mixed animal clinic for years. I've seen stud bulls and stallions flaunt more in the way of family jewels than you'll ever own, Dr. Hart. Drop it."

After a moment, he muttered truculently, "All right, all right," and threw the quilt off.

More than all right. She squashed that thought and coaxed him with her hands at his hips into leaning heavily on both her and the crutch.

There it was again, Trip thought with a start when her hands pressed into his flesh. That strange something that had seemed to flow from her touch earlier was streaming through him again. His pain seemed to lessen to only half what it had been a moment before. He sucked in a breath as the sensation prodded another memory. If the potent response her touch had provoked before became reality right now—

"Careful now. Just lean on me," she said. It wasn't easy to bear his weight while not touching his bound ribs. She had to cup a steadying hand around his bare right buttock as he balanced precariously beside her.

"I've got it now. You wait in the hall. I'll holler if I need anything." *You know what you'll need if she doesn't get her hands off you. Mind over matter, man. Get your back to her, get into the john and don't let her touch you again unless you want to be truly overexposed.*

Brenna told herself it was the doctor in her that noted how firm his bottom was to the touch as her hand left him. No atrophied muscles after a two-week stint flat on his back for the man who had formerly shucked his clothes off in two moves? How had he maintained rock-hard buns in the hospital? Isometrics in bed?

Brenna hovered a fingertip away from him as he tottered into the bathroom adjacent to his closet. When he pivoted slightly to slam the door, her last glimpse of him gave her something to ponder that rivaled his buns for hardness.

On legs that felt not wholly functional, she moved into the hall and stood there. In the silence, her thumping heart and racing blood relayed a message it would have taken a lot of self-deception to ignore. She was turned on, flushed hot by what she had glimpsed.

As broken up as he was, Trip remained an obviously virile and attractive man. Brenna breathed out a long, shaky sigh. Even before she had met him in the flesh, she had fantasized about him. Here, in the flesh, he was doubly exciting.

She could safely say she hadn't felt this physically affected by a man for years. Maybe never. Her attraction to her husband had leaned more to the cerebral than either the physical or emotional.

For Trip, though, she felt—what? She squeezed her trembling thighs together at the sensual warmth her mental inquiry evoked. There was no question of her physical response to him. After her first glance at his portrait, she hadn't been able to deny a yearning to finally meet him, touch him. Now that they had met and touched, she was devastated. She had to also admit a yearning to plumb the mix of emotions her imagination had fueled.

His irascible disposition earlier hadn't lessened the longing. All evening she had pondered his behavior, deciding it was a necessary defense mechanism against his feeling helpless, powerless, emasculated by all that had happened to him. Somewhere underneath was the Trip Hart she had come to know from living in his home, knowing his mother, working his practice, meeting his clients.

The people in this far-flung community all respected and admired Trip Hart. Some even adored him. He hadn't been gruff and gritty for long.

"Hey, Brenna," he called from the bathroom.

She jumped as if he'd touched her right where she was warmest. "Yes?"

"Bring me a clean pair of shorts, would you? Please. Top dresser drawer on the right."

She hurried into his room and pulled a pair from the designated drawer, feeling suddenly tactless. Why didn't *you* think of that first, she chided herself. Give the poor man a break in a pinch. She slipped the shorts through the crack he'd opened in the door.

After it closed again, she heard a sharp, "Damn."

Now she knew why she hadn't thought of it. He couldn't bend at the waist with his ribs bound.

"Forget the shorts," she called in. "Wrap a towel around you if it matters that much."

"I can't make one stay on. Damned cast . . ." was his muffled answer.

Brenna folded her arms over her chest and regarded the bathroom door. "Trip, I have two hands to your one. I can help." When he didn't answer, she added, "It shouldn't matter that much, you know. You're not the first man I've seen nude. I was married to one once upon a time and I've had a fling with one or two since."

He cracked the door. "Not with me, you haven't."

"Trip, for heaven's sake, we're both doctors."

"Don't give me that stallion routine again. I'm not making any more special appearances and that's that."

Brenna rolled her eyes. "How many nurses did you have at the hospital?"

"Too damn many."

"Did you give *them* this bad a time?"

"Did I ever. I also did them a favor. I left a week early."

"Trust me, Trip. You're blowing this way out of proportion."

"Trust me, Trip," he mocked in a cartoon falsetto before he fell back into his own deep baritone. "If you're so trustworthy, put your money where your mouth is."

"How?"

"Drop your nightie, *señorita*, and show me *your* stuff without a blush."

"I—I don't have to." Brenna tightened the tie belt on her robe nevertheless. "I'm not the one who can't get dressed alone because of a couple of casts and a bruised set of ribs."

"What if you were?"

"If I—" She had an image of herself hanging on Trip and a crutch, his hand cupped to her bare bottom, her breasts bared to his dark-hot gaze. "I'd get real about it real fast," she lied. "Skin is skin."

"I heard that beat you missed," he retorted. "Gave you something to think about, didn't I? Sure, skin is skin, *señorita*, but when it's your own pretty hide it's a different story. Trust you? Ha!"

"Look, Trip. I'm not dropping my nightgown just so we can be twinsies when I tuck you back into bed. Be practical."

"Who says you're tucking me in?"

As much as the idea made her curl her bare toes in anticipation, she too had to be practical. "At this point, I'd like to throw you out a window for being so childish. Grow up, Trip. If you can't get out of bed without me, you can't get back in without me."

"Hey, you don't have to insist on following me in, *señorita*. You're welcome in my bed anytime. I may be a cripple, but I'm not blind."

Though she knew her slip had been Freudian, she felt compelled to insist, "That's not what I meant by 'without me,' Trip."

"I know." There was a moment of silence behind the door before his tone segued from mildly sarcastic to scornful. "I know it's not. Hell, you're not blind, either. What woman would welcome a night in bed with Trip the Crip?"

Brenna fought back the surge of pity that rose in her at the desolate expression she sensed he wore as he spoke those bleak words. She knew her sympathy would do him no good. It was his pity for himself he had to battle.

"Who, indeed?" she retorted as caustically as she knew she must. "I can't think of anyone but Bleeding Heart Brenna. She might be able to force herself if you begged hard enough."

It was the only way. Anger was his sole weapon now against the aching vulnerability, regret and depression he had yet to overcome. For his sake, she had to fuel his fury, pretend he was every bit the nasty man he truly needed to be to survive this critical stage on his road to recovery.

It worked. He yanked the door open, his eyes as fierce as she could have hoped.

"Thanks for the offer, dear *heart*, but this beggar isn't a charity case." He tossed her his shorts. "Now, get me into these as fast as you got me out of them."

4

"SORRY ABOUT THAT."

"Forget being sorry, Trip."

"Forget. Sure. You'd think I'd been shot full of aphrodisiacs instead of painkillers for two weeks." Propped against pillows and headboard, Trip bent his good knee to tent the bedcovers over his hips and watched Brenna clean up the broken lamp.

"I'm not offended."

"Why is your face as red as chili salsa, then?"

"I'm blushing *for* you, not *at* you." With trembling fingers that belied her reasonable tone, Brenna tossed the last of the glass shards and fragments into a wicker wastebasket and stood, as ready to change the subject as Trip was to reproach himself. "Have you had anything to eat today?"

"No."

"Are you hungry?"

"Starved." And not just for food, he thought, slanting a half-lidded glance down at her long, bare legs.

"So am I. I'll throw together a snack. Is there anything you can't have?"

"Only the fun stuff—like a glass of the jug of red wine in the pantry, if you could pour me one." Painkiller, aphrodisiac, B. J. Deveney was both, all rolled up into one sexy nightshirted female. The sooner she headed to the kitchen for food and wine, the better.

"Coming right up." Clutching the wastebasket against her breathless chest, unwilling to argue that she suspected his doctor had forbidden him alcohol in any form, Brenna rushed her blazing face into the kitchen.

By the time she returned balancing a full tray, she was as calm and composed as she supposed any nurse of Trip Hart's could get with a patient like him under the covers. She set the tray on the empty side of his bed and pulled up a chair, relieved to see that he, too, had calmed a nerve or two in her absence. His good leg was flat on the mattress again.

He stared at the tray with eyebrows raised in surprise. "Cheese omelets? This is some snack."

"You said you were starved."

"Make that voracious. I've almost forgotten what real food looks like. They don't serve it in the hospital, that's for sure." He lifted the glass of red wine she handed him. "To my relief vet . . . thanks for playing nurse."

She clinked his glass with hers. "Thanks for admitting you need one. She's not up on the latest techniques, but she's doing her best."

"I won't need one for long, if it's worrying you," he said, shooting her a quick, dark look.

"I'm not worried." She placed his plate on his lap. "But I'm more certain than ever that I didn't miss my calling when I chose to doctor animals instead of humans."

"Thanks a lot from the only other human in a twenty-five-mile radius."

"You're welcome. From what I can see, you didn't miss your calling, either. How would you like to have *you* as a patient?"

"I'd rather arm-wrestle a gorilla," he said, after a long pause in which the thunderheads dispersed from his gaze. "Can you stand me until my mother shows up again?"

"Only if we get a few things straight between us."

His eyes darkened again. "Things like me being Mr. Congeniality instead of Attila the Hun, I suppose?"

"More of one and less of the other wouldn't hurt." She shrugged. "Actually, the problem isn't that you roar like a lion and swear like a stevedore. I'd probably do the same if I were you."

"What do we need to get straight, then?"

"The issue of help, first. You need it. I offer it. You have no choice until Lita comes back on Tuesday. Please accept a helping hand without waging a major battle every time. All right?"

"I'll give it a try." Another long pause. "What else?"

"You might have to try twice as hard on this one. Lita says you're convinced that she's matchmaking. She's not. And if, by some chance, she's fooled even me, you can relax. I didn't come out here to get matched up. I came to work, and I'd like to stay on unless you object for some other reason." Brenna frowned and cut into her omelet. "You've got a nice setup, and I think Lita and your clients will vouch that I've done a competent job of keeping it afloat these past two weeks. I need the work and I like this place. Do I leave tomorrow or stay as long as you need a relief vet?"

"You don't mince words, do you?"

"Not when I have rent to pay on my house in San Jose. I have bills like everyone else, too. Do I stay or go?"

A very long pause. "Stay."

"We're on," she said around a mouthful of omelet.

"Is that it, then?" He set his glass on the tray and picked up his fork.

"Not quite." Brenna took a long swig of wine before continuing, "As doctors, we both know that physical reflexes are a fact of life. All of them—male and female—

voluntary and involuntary are perfectly natural. Your reflex a while ago was simply a . . . a . . ."

He looked almost appalled as her search for words sent color to her cheeks that had nothing to do with her ingestion of red wine. Even as she inwardly cursed the involuntary reaction, though, it presented the perfect simile to her struggling tongue.

"What happened was like a blush," she continued quickly. "I'm blushing . . . and you blushed. I can't help it now and you couldn't help it then. I can't promise I won't do it again and neither can you. We're even. No apologies on either side, now or in the future."

Trip was monumentally glad his mouth was full. It saved him from staring at her with it hanging open. It saved him from assembling a response as tactful yet direct as the words she'd just spoken. It saved him from doing anything else but nodding in hesitant agreement as he chewed the most delicious mouthful of herb-and-cheese omelet he'd ever tasted. It took a lot of chewing before he could swallow. A bracing gulp of wine followed before he could form an answer.

"You know, Doctor," he managed at last, "you may have missed your calling, after all. You have all the makings of a crack diplomat."

Brenna looked up from the plate on her lap and felt her omelet fold over on itself in her stomach. The smile on his lips was a charming, vulnerable curve that warmed more than her cheeks. She felt suddenly like a furled red rose soaking up sunshine from petals to stem to roots. At one upcurved corner of Trip's mouth a deep dimple flashed, rousing an immediate, irrational desire in her to test its minuscule, conical depth with the tip of her tongue.

You want this man, an inner voice stated with utter conviction. *You've wanted him ever since you set eyes on his portrait in the parlor two weeks ago. Everything you've learned about him since has only reinforced it.* She curled her fingers around her plate and flicked her gaze from his smile to his bare chest to her own bare knees. Pressed tightly together, her knees were flushing along with her cheeks. *Ay, Chihuahua.*

"Your omelet's getting cold. Eat up," she heard herself say, unsure whether it was Trip's ears or her own that her soft brusque command had been meant for.

Yes, eat instead of making her squirm in her chair at your dopey comments and dopier grin, you fool, Trip told himself. If he kept on grinning and blushing like a girl-crazy fourteen-year-old, she'd be laughing herself back to sleep tonight. This wasn't the time to forget he was no longer the most eligible lone-wolf bachelor in the county.

Nice time to realize she's a woman you might have stopped being a confirmed bachelor for. Heck of a time now that you're a man a desirable woman wouldn't look at twice.

He forced his fork from his plate to his mouth, regretting with each awkward move that he hadn't been born left-handed. Down and up his hand and fork made their unsteady journey until his plate was clean and Brenna had stopped looking as if escape at the first opportunity was a brilliant idea.

"You like San Jose?" Trip asked, watching her eat.

She nodded. "It's growing too fast, but that's exciting in its own way. The microchip industry fuels the economy and there's a clash between the small-towners and the upscale high-techies. Never a dull moment."

"Which side are you on?"

"Neither. I grew up in a small town in Iowa. Too small. Too much corn. My parents pulled up stakes when I was sixteen and moved to San Jose where my uncle had a huge wholesale plant nursery. A few years later, they got homesick for the cornfields and moved back. I stayed on at UC Davis where I was going to college and settled in San Jose after my divorce. I rent a little house outside of town where it's zoned for livestock—such as two Chinese Potbelly Miniatures."

It was a relief to see her expression switch from pained to politely conversational. He'd have to watch himself, he decided. He thought of how pained Brenna would be if she knew the extent to which she'd occupied his thoughts from that first moment in the parlor. It was insane, this sudden yearning to do all the things with her that he hadn't done for so long with any woman, no matter how desirable and attractive the female.

Nevertheless he yearned to flirt outrageously with this one, date her, seduce her, court her, woo her into his arms, his bed, his life. If she knew, she'd bolt straight out of that chair and back to San Jose.

She'd be polite enough not to laugh in his face, of course, even if she suspected. As polite as she had been with that brave little speech about erections and blushes. As polite as she was being right now, avoiding his eyes, clearing the plates and glasses onto the tray, pretending he hadn't looked like a three-year-old when he fed himself. No, she wouldn't laugh outright and point out how incapable he was of anything more than a kiss and a one-armed hug.

Like she said, she needs a paycheck. Right now that includes putting up with the boss until his mother comes back on Tuesday. You're the one who reminded her right off who was in charge around here, Boss Man.

"How long have you been a vet?" he found himself asking, as if it weren't as clear as Himalayan air that she'd like to leave with the tray as soon as possible.

"Close to five years. What about you?" She rose, moved the tray to her vacated wooden chair and sat down on the bed where the tray had been to await his answer.

"What about . . . me?" For an astonished second, Trip felt moved to think he'd been wrong about romance remaining a feature of the distant past for him. Here it was, sitting on his bed like a gorgeous gift from heaven.

"I mean, how long have you been practicing?" Brenna knew his entire professional history from Lita, but hearing it from those lips with the smile dimple in the corner would be like hearing it again for the first time.

It was her tone of polite inquiry, devoid of any trace of seduction, that pulled Trip back from giddy wonder to planet Earth. The real wonder was how a man as helpless as a baby could interpret her transfer from a hard chair to a softer seat on his bed as anything more than it appeared. She would never have sat herself down like that on the bed of an able-bodied man.

"Let's see, I've been in business twice that long. My father and I partnered the practice for a year together before he died. He built it up from scratch and left it all to me, so I can't claim more than keeping it going."

Brenna knew he was understating facts. Lita had already described how Trip had improved and expanded the practice to where he would soon have to either hire an associate or turn down new patients. She didn't dispute him, however. It was too nice to engage in something besides battle with him. Something she recognized as really no different from first-date conversation. Something she hadn't had in a long time. Even rarer was second-date conversation. Most of the men she'd met in the past few years hadn't rated a second round. Those who did rarely rated a third.

"Have you been doing relief work long?" he asked.

"No. I was a full-time clinic vet until a few months ago. The partnership I was counting on after six years didn't pan out." She hoped he wouldn't ask why, adding, "I decided to free-lance until I found something that *would* work out and here I am."

Trip shook his head. "I couldn't be content with relief work. My roots—my family's roots—run deep here in these hills, and I like running my own show too much to run anyone else's. Not that I'm criticizing. Who am I to criticize? How many vets have an established practice waiting for them when they graduate from vet school? I was lucky."

"Yes," Brenna agreed, "but luck doesn't keep a practice on its feet, much less expand it. That takes dedication and vision and talent. From what I've seen of your practice, you've done your father proud." Her reward for that well-deserved compliment was a reluctant aw-shucks grin from him that encouraged her to say, "I'll be proud to add your recommendation to my list of satisfied clients, too, if you're satisfied when I'm through here."

Trip's grin faded and he looked down at his arm cast. "By the time you're through here, I'll be through here, too."

"Lita says that's not a certainty," Brenna objected, wishing she hadn't inadvertently raised the painful issue. "Your cast isn't even off yet. There's no telling what might—"

Trip held up a hand. "*Might* and *will* are two different species of word. The odds for *might* are a hundred to one.

Will isn't even in the vocabulary. If I can't handle any size animal and do surgery, I'm dead on the dime as a country vet. Don't pull the Pollyanna routine with me, Doctor. I know what the prognosis is, and it isn't—"

What stopped him in midsentence were Brenna's legs as she swung them up onto the bed and jackknifed them horizontally in front of her, calves aligned with thighs. She pulled her short robe to her knees and said, "Go on. I'm just getting entrenched for the rest of my Pollyanna routine. What is it that your prognosis is not?"

"It's not—" his eyes felt permanently focused on her slender, lightly freckled calves "—ringed with rainbows." Never had minuscule freckles dusted on the surface of any other skin been quite the visual draw her legs had just become.

Brenna traced a fingertip around and around one patchwork square on the quilt as she pressed her argument. "How can you say that even a one percent chance shouldn't have an equal percentage of hope attached to it? How long has it been since your last lesson in logic, Trip?"

The sole question in Trip's mind was how long had it been since he'd been anything but alone in his bed. Brenna sat close enough that he could have stroked his able hand from her knees to her pink-polished toe tips without straining a muscle. Close enough that he could have captured her moving hand in his and kissed the finger so familiar now with that patch on his quilt. If he wanted to.

He wanted to. More than anything else at that moment, he wanted to stroke and capture and kiss until she slipped between the sheets with him, heedless of his every disability.

"Too long to remember the particulars," he answered, catching her soap-fresh scent. To keep himself from doing what he wanted, he touched his hand to his bandaged head and said, "The old memory bank hasn't been quite the same since the concussion, I'm afraid."

Brenna's expression veered swiftly from earnest indignation to earnest concern. "Does it hurt?"

"Only during the opening act of a Pollyanna routine."

Her concern shifted sideways to sneaking suspicion. "Are you faking a headache so I'll shut up?"

"No. It just started up again, without any warning."

"I'm sorry if what I said started it."

"It didn't. My head's been aching off and on for two weeks, whenever it feels like it. Right now, it's on." Solely due to the rampage of thoughts in his head about her legs, he was quite certain.

"Is there anything you can take for it?"

"Yes, but no thanks. I'm sicker of being doped up than I am of hurting off and on. After two weeks of living in a twilight zone, there's something to be said for knowing exactly how I feel."

"If there's anything I can do . . ."

"Try talking to me—about something besides hope, if you can. It might take my mind off the pain." *And keep you here beside me until I can stand the thought of you leaving for your own bed.*

Every word of first-date talk she'd ever concocted over a dinner table deserted her as she sat there, wishing she could reach out and touch him, lie beside him and comfort him in her arms.

"What would you like to talk about?" she had to finally ask after an unproductive silence.

"Anything." It was obvious she'd rather argue the illogical logic of hope than engage in forced chitchat, but beggars couldn't afford to be choosy. "Ask a question. Any question."

She thought for a moment. "Okay. What's your head bandage for?" *Brilliant, Brenna. Ask a man who wants to forget his aching head what's under the bandage around it.*

"A scalp cut that took ten stitches to close." The same number of delicate toes on her shapely feet, and fingers on her graceful hands. "They were going to take the bandage off for good today at the hospital, but I escaped before they got to me."

"Maybe the bandage is giving you a headache," she offered. "I always get one when I wear a ski hat. Would you like me to cut it off? It might help."

Oh, he'd like. She'd have to get closer, female and soap fresh, to snip and unwind the long gauze strip. Closer would be heaven. Hell would be the reaction she'd have to the jagged and slowly healing cut on the right side of his head. A wide swath of his hair had been shaved off there, leaving him resembling nothing so much as a punk rock star or a circus clown under the bandage.

"I don't think so," he delayed with a fake fuzzy smile. "Maybe tomorrow after I've rested up." Paycheck or no paycheck, one look at his creep-show head and she'd scoot off the bed for good. Keeping her there beside him had become the most important thing in the world.

Brenna tried not to look as disappointed as she felt at his clear reluctance to invite her touch. He would only let her get so close and no closer. Closer was what she wanted. It was almost as if he knew what she wanted and wanted none of the same. Alarm bells went off in her mind as that thought made headway. Had he guessed? Was it in her eyes for him to see? Oh, please, not there for him to see and reject like the ill-fated housekeepers Lita had so optimistically hired.

"Good grief," she exclaimed with a start. "That's what you need more than small talk, isn't it? Rest." She unfolded and slid off the bed. "Here I am yakking away and you've just been too polite to yawn. You're tired and—"

"I'm not a bit tir—"

"Of course you are. Who wouldn't be? So am I, come to think of it." She grabbed the tray. "I'll just get this out of your way so you can get some sleep."

Trip slumped back and watched her sail through the door with the tray. As decisions went, his choice to delay had proven the dumbest ever. One word would have kept her close, touching him, filling his head with the most erotic of soap-scented fantasies even as she exposed his punk haircut to her inevitable disgust.

Yes. The simplest of words. Why hadn't he said it and suffered the consequences? Double dumb. The agony at the end would have been worth the ecstasy of getting there.

"Dumb, dumb, dumb," Brenna muttered at herself during her quick cleanup in the kitchen. She hadn't meant to sit down on his bed. But her legs had walked her right over and plopped her down on it. They'd have slid themselves right between his sheets, too, with enough encouragement from him.

That was the worst of it. His evasive manner indicated he knew how ready and willing she was. How could he not know? A woman didn't make herself comfortable on a man's bed without signaling a definite message to him. He'd received the message and returned it unopened. Any woman with half an IQ could have seen his total lack of romantic interest, despite his propensity to blush at the drop of a fig leaf.

Knowing she'd been ready to come on to a man who'd exhibited no respone to her beyond being hugely embarrassed at being physically exposed made her cringe inside. How much did he suspect? She winced at the thought. Never had she come on to a man. She'd never had to before now. Now she wished she had taken the initiative at least once before this in her adult life. An ounce of experience would have saved her a pound of cringing in the kitchen.

Her great hope at the moment was that he'd been hurting too much to dwell on what she'd done. A greater hope was that he'd be asleep by the time she skulked back into his bedroom to hook up another bedside lamp and place his crutch where he could reach it. By tomorrow morning, if she adopted a frosty outer attitude, he might even conclude he'd been imagining things.

To her relief, when she tiptoed in with the lamp, he announced, "I can't sleep with a head like this. You've got to do something—besides taking off the bandage."

This was better, she thought. If he'd concluded she'd gotten the message and he had nothing more to worry about, he was one hundred percent correct. From now on, she'd act like Florence Nightingale instead of a sex-starved divorcée. No more wine in the wee hours of the morning, either. The last thing she needed in his presence was a weakening influence.

"Maybe some aspirin would help," she suggested briskly.

"I doubt it."

"Try it or hire another nurse." There. Her tone had been tough and no-nonsense. Nurse-perfect. He wouldn't catch *her* invading his personal space again.

The act succeeded. He swallowed the three aspirins his bathroom medicine cabinet yielded and let her help him slide down from the headboard to lie flat on his back.

"I still don't think aspirin's going to do the trick," he said as he settled into his pillow.

"What did they give you in the hospital?"

"A shot, whether I wanted one or not." He shrugged and gave her a wan smile. "But my nurse used to massage my forehead until it took hold." That the latter was a total fabrication was his last concern. Inveigling small favors without being caught at it was his first.

Brenna made no reply. If he wanted a no-nonsense message, he could ask for it like the no-nonsense patient he'd so subtly informed her he wanted to remain.

"Would you mind?" he asked.

Mind? Ten minutes ago, she would have leaped tall buildings at the chance. Now she gave the question the grave consideration Florence N. would have granted it and decided no nurse worth her starched white cap would refuse to ease a patient's pain at his own request.

"Whatever you'd like," she replied. There was nothing to mind in leaving everything to him.

Just mind your manners, Ms. Nightingale, an inner voice interjected. *Your bedside manner, in particular. And pray that your hands don't suddenly decide to do their thing on the spur of the moment tonight. They already lost you most of what you wanted out of life. Don't add Trip Hart to the loss column.*

Brenna raised her hands to look at them. They looked perfectly normal, capable, harmless. Just looking at them, no one would ever know they were capable of instilling fear in others. Even her palmist grandmother had never read anything untoward in them, though Brenna *had* felt that Gram hadn't revealed everything she'd seen in her granddaughter's palms. Brenna wished she could talk to her, but Gram was dead and couldn't be consulted now.

Brenna's only consultation had been with her doctor and the psychiatrist. Neither had any answers for her. The psychiatrist, however, had made an offhand suggestion that Brenna might want to talk to a woman who was a test subject in a unique study at a nearby university research lab.

Howmedica Plant was a fifty-year-old Englishwoman whose sea-foam green eyes were jewel bright with an inner smile and whose frizzy red hair stood almost on end. An hour spent with Howmedica convinced Brenna that the woman was psychic, if nothing else. But she was more.

"And so you read palms, I see," Howmedica had said without preamble when Brenna met her for coffee at the university student union. "Your Gram taught you. She never did tell you *everything*, did she?"

To Brenna's astounded expression, Howmedica had cheerfully replied, "I also see auras, the colorful energy fields around people. Yours has a great deal of whitish gray in it, my dear. You fear what is happening to you. I did, too, when my time came unannounced. You mustn't be afraid. Let the light come and go as it will and in time it takes a favored path. Mustn't draw the shades and huddle inside, hiding your own light. No. Open wide the door. Let love and light pour in and out. It's the only way to go, my dear."

"Something wrong?" Trip inquired, his eyes open, searching hers.

"No," Brenna said quickly, brushing her palms together as if dusting her thoughts away. "I was just wondering how your nurse did it."

"Did what?"

"I mean—" Brenna moved around to his side of the bed, mystified by whatever logistics his nurse had employed "—where did she sit?"

"Behind me." One subterfuge after another and now he was in too deep to dig out. "She, er, rolled my hospital bed out and cranked it down and, uh...massaged."

"This is no bed on wheels," was Brenna's nurselike observation, "but I think we can manage if you scoot down and I sit Indian-style with your pillow in my lap." Never let it be said that he had no say. "How does that strike you?"

It struck him like the brainstorm of the century, despite the fact that she didn't look very enamored of her own idea. "That sounds like a plan," he agreed as calmly as he could. His head in her lap. A godsend.

Backed up against the oak headboard with Trip's head in her pillowed lap, Brenna wondered if she shouldn't have pleaded fatigue and left him with his suspicions and his headache. Now there was no turning back. She pressed her palms together. They felt only warm, not hot. Nothing animated them tonight other than her yearning to touch the man and gaze down into his face to her heart's content. At the first sign of heat, if it came, she'd snatch her hands away, plead fatigue like she should have when he first uttered the word "massage."

"Ahhh, that's what she did," Trip sighed when she gently rotated his temples with her fingertips. "That's even better than she did."

"Tell me if I hurt you any more than you're hurting already."

"I will. Mmm, you're not hurting."

Trip felt both guilty and grateful as he lay there. Guilty for taking advantage of what was every true veterinarian's natural desire to ease any pain, heal any hurt. Grateful for the magic spell Brenna's fingers were weaving. Guilty for manipulating an employer's advantage over an employee. Most grateful for the clean scent of her skin so intense now in his nostrils that he could almost taste it.

"How am I doing?" she asked, stroking his forehead as she recalled hers had been stroked during the facials she'd sometimes indulged in at a skin salon.

Trip could only nod his reply. He feared that if he opened his mouth, the truth would come out on a blissful sigh. *You're doing everything just right. You're beautiful, sexy, sassy, smart. You have the touch of an angel and eyes that could brighten even heaven with a glance. If I were what I once was, I'd get on intimate terms with your heart and mind and every freckle on your body starting yesterday. Where were you when I was what I was? Where have you been until now?*

Encouraged by his nod, Brenna let her fingertips spiral down from Trip's temples to the shadowy stubble of beard at his jaw. She gazed down at his closed eyes, at the crescent shadows his thick lashes threw on his cheeks in the lamplight. His lips were full, slightly parted. Her massaging fingers stilled for a moment as she thought about how his mouth might feel fused to hers. She squeezed her eyes shut. Don't look. Don't think.

"Don't stop."

Brenna's eyes flashed open at his soft murmured directive. She watched, unmoving, as Trip's left hand came up to lightly cover hers. It seemed like a dream when he pressed her fingertips to his lips in a silent plea that she continue. Her only thought when he released her was that his mouth was as smoldering as the slow burn that lived in his dark eyes. Branded with the memory of his lips, her fingers longed to move on in hot little circles over his shoulders down to the flat copper-brown nipples on his chest.

She felt her breath back into itself and then slam to a halt as her hands warmed. Was it happening again? Or was it simply a reaction to the warmth of his kiss and the smoldering thoughts in her mind? Either way, she couldn't afford it. Quick! She pulled her hands away.

"Wha—?"

"A leg cramp," she lied hastily. "Stay still. I'll just slide out from under and walk it off." In a matter of seconds, she was on her feet, saying, "I never *could* sit like Pocahontas for very long without kinking up."

"A squaw-style message was your idea, not mine." Trip scowled to conceal the frustration and self-rebuke that vied for top dog in his constricted chest. He inched back up to his former position and shot her a dark frown.

She feigned a limp to the door and paused there. "I'm sorry to just leave you like this, but—I *am* awfully tired and this cramp is—"

"Tell me about it in the morning. I'm tired, you're tired, everybody's beat. You don't have to stand there wringing your hands and cramping up all over the place. Walk it off on your way back to bed."

"You'll be okay?"

"My trusty crutch and I can make it through the next few hours," he said curtly. "Kill the overhead light on your way out, would you?"

She flipped the switch. "I'm right down the hall if you need anything."

"For anything except the shortest massage in history, I'll 'roar like a lion and swear like a stevedore.'"

"I said I was sorry." Brenna clenched her burning hands at her sides.

"Try saying good-night like a good nurse and score a bonus point with the patient."

Damn him. If he could be a difficult, obstinate patient, his volunteer nurse could get difficult, too. "I scored more than a few points with dinner and aspirin. And short as it was, you got more of a massage than I've given anyone in years," she pointed out. "Try scoring a bonus of your own with a single thank-you for my time and trouble."

"My stomach appreciates it very much, but my head isn't quite up to it, yet. Is that singular enough for you?"

"Enough to make me want to push that crutch just out of your reach," Brenna fumed, "and let you ponder your next move without it—and me."

"Touch it and die, Dr. Deveney." He switched out his lamp.

"You'll eat those words when nature calls again, Dr. Hart."

SUNDAY DAWNED A SCORCHER. It was eighty degrees and rising at nine o'clock when Brenna woke to the ring of the extension phone next to her bed.

She fumbled the receiver to her ear only to hear Trip on his own extension say, "I've got it," while a voice on the other end identified himself as Everett Jamison, Trip's doctor at the hospital.

She hung up and got out of bed, rubbing the sleep out of her eyes and wishing she could eavesdrop on the conversation. Trip couldn't be counted on to relay a full and satisfactory account of the doctor's instructions for his patient's conduct and care while at home. But that could wait. A phone call to the doctor from Lita would fill in the gaps.

Receiver to his ear, Trip looked up when she stood in his doorway in her nightshirt and short robe. Brenna pointed at the bathroom door and raised her eyebrows. He pointed at the phone and rolled his eyes, a sign she interpreted as time enough for a quick shower and a blow-dry before he'd need her.

Trip was just returning the receiver to its cradle when Brenna reentered in a pair of white shorts and her yellow terry tube top from the day before. If he wanted a nurse's uniform, he could hire one, she had decided as she dressed. He could think whatever he liked about her summer attire. Whether he was home or not, she would have worn what she was wearing. She'd let a cool, correct demeanor inform him that she had dressed for the summer heat and not for him.

"How's the head?" she asked.

"Off again. The aspirin last night helped."

"Sleep well?"

"Better than in the hospital."

"What did Jamison have to say?"

"Not much that can be repeated to a lady. What *can* be repeated is rest, rest and rest until he drives out to see me on Tuesday."

"No prescriptions for anything?"

"Nothing I don't have in my own pharmacy if I need it."

"Speaking of needs—" she nodded in the direction of the bathroom "—would you like to wash up?"

"An idea whose moment has come. Now that I've had time to ponder my next move at excruciating length, you can touch my crutch."

Brenna spared him a curt snicker. "I *thought* you might see things differently in the bright light of day."

The only things Trip was seeing differently in the morning light were Brenna's breasts. Point-blank they were even more heart stopping than they had been at a distance the day before, firm and round and crowned with nipples poised in a soft pout. His swift assessment left him quite certain that nature had shaped her to fit so precisely in his hands there wouldn't have been an extra pinch of flesh left over if he cupped his palms to her.

"Heave ho. Here we go." Brenna positioned the crutch for him and bore his weight as he struggled up to balance on it. He was steadier this time, less uncertain of his movements, and was lumbering off on his own before she quite realized it.

"Not bad for a beginner, huh?" he exulted when he made it to the bathroom door unaided. "I'll bet I can even manage a shave and a one-handed sponge bath if I give it the old vet-school try."

Brenna couldn't help smiling with her own exultation. He looked pleased with himself for the first time since he'd come home. With further successful attempts at autonomy, she hoped he'd cheer up more. In time, he might even be able to summon forth a laugh. Though with his ribs in a body bandage, she could see why he might now have some reluctance to even take a really deep breath, much less chuckle.

"Why don't you just do that, then," she said. "I'll make breakfast. How do you like your eggs?"

"Sunny-side up on a bed of hot salsa with tortillas, if you haven't eaten them all."

"Lita brought in reinforcements yesterday."

"If she brought coffee, too, perk up a big pot." He started to shut the door, but paused to ask over his shoulder, "Would you circle around in a few minutes to wash my back?"

"No problem." She almost choked on the two words. "How do you like your coffee?"

"Black and strong. And thanks for your time and trouble from here on in." He shut the door before she could answer.

In the kitchen, Brenna snagged the yolks of two eggs on their split shells and spilled half a can of coffee on the counter before she pulled herself back into proper enough shape to retrace her steps to his room after the few minutes he'd requested. On the journey, she did what little she could to banish the dark shadow of his morning beard from her mind.

Imagining that raspy stubble grazing over her lips and breasts had been enough to scatter coffee grounds to the four winds. Given that, and what the afterimage of Trip in his shorts could do to scramble eggs he'd ordered unscrambled, she hated to think what havoc the process of washing his back might wreak.

She tried to take some comfort in the fact that her no-nonsense behavior seemed to have assured Trip she wouldn't take up where she'd cut off her foray onto his bed last night. He'd never have offered his back if he hadn't been sure of it. She'd have liked to feel as confident of herself as he so apparently did.

He was facing the washbasin with his face lathered up for a shave when she got there. That helped the morning-shadow problem. The musky, masculine scent of his shave cream canceled out the help. As did the fact that he'd managed to unhook and unwind the corset bandage from his ribs.

"Aren't you supposed to be bound up for a while longer?" she asked with an aplomb worthy of a woman who hadn't noticed he looked like a magazine ad for men's underwear, despite his shaving lather and arm and leg casts. Even the purplish bruises around his ribs didn't detract from the virile image.

"Not according to Jamison this morning. Thank God, he caved in over the corset. I hate being wrapped up in that damned thing. Here." He handed her a washcloth wrung out in hot water and leaned hard upon the washbasin with his left hand.

With eyes averted from her reflection over his shoulder in the mirror, Brenna bathed him with light strokes that were careful of his bruises and burns but didn't linger on the smooth muscles under his skin or the tapering planes from his shoulders to his waist.

"Easy on the burns," he warned at one point. "You don't know how good that feels," he murmured at another.

One thing she knew for certain was how perfectly smooth his olive skin was down to the waist of his shorts and surely between there and his thighs. In contrast to her dotted-swiss cheese epidermis, his had not a mark on it except for bruises and a few slow-healing burns. Unlike freckles, those would disappear with time. The day science discovered how to zap freckles, she intended to be the first zappee.

Trip searched her expression in the mirror for a sign that she didn't resent this added chore he'd foisted on her along with breakfast. Because she was almost as tall as he, he could see her face clearly behind him as she rinsed and dried him off. Whatever she was thinking wasn't apparent, for she kept her eyes down.

Had she been admiring his tush, he could have harbored a slim hope that she might come to admire the few other good points he had left. Only the stoic set of her bowed pink lips offered a clue to her lack of anything but a clinical interest in her task. Her words as she finished with him confirmed it.

"Do you have something medicated for burns?"

"Just this." He opened the medicine cabinet and produced a white jar.

She read the label. "This is for chapped udders. Don't you have anything else?"

Deserting hope completely, he sighed, "Just rub it on and pretend I'm a cow. It works for chapped hands and faces as well as milk bags. I guarantee it'll smooth out a few scrapes on a cripple."

"Stop calling yourself that or you won't get your way with anything *I* have any control over." Brenna gave herself a mental pat on the back. Florence couldn't have said it better.

"Okay, I'll stop. Now rub it on."

He said it harshly enough that she complied, but not without comment. "No more of that Trip-the-Crip stuff, either."

"Fine. Just keep the cream coming. I can feel it working already." After a moment, he said, "What's wrong with Trip the Crip? It has a certain poetic ring to it, don't you think?"

"You mean the ring of self-pity I hear whenever you say it? Somehow I didn't expect you'd be the self-pitying type."

"Oh?" His shoulder tightened under her hands. "And how long have you been drawing conclusions about my character and emotional makeup?"

"Ever since I got here," Brenna said, administering a final dab of cream and thanking heaven that the medicinal smell had drowned out the heady scent of Trip's shave cream. "I concluded right away that no one whose first thought was for himself would have risked life and limb to save a wild animal from a horrible death."

"Would it change your mind if I—" he stared down into the washbasin "—if I said I almost regret having done that, now?"

Brenna capped the cream jar and set it aside. "'Almost' is a telling word," she said firmly. "I don't believe you'll ever regret saving that deer."

"Maybe not," he conceded with a catch in his voice. "Maybe I don't regret what I did, maybe I never will. But you can believe that I damn sure regret being only half the man I was two weeks ago."

Brenna forced herself to make no response to the dark pain she saw in his eyes in the mirror. Acknowledging it would only tempt her to wrap her arms around him and press her lips and breasts against his bruised back in mute testimony that not only was he the most courageous, desirable man she had ever met but she was getting emotionally involved so fast it was frightening.

She wondered if she was falling in love and felt dizzy at the possibility. She was grateful her face didn't reflect the inner heat of her reaction to Trip. It had kindled at first sight of his portrait, smoldered for two weeks, then flared to flame in the whirlwind of his unexpected arrival home.

Fanning the flame to fire was something she knew she couldn't afford to do unless Trip made a U-turn on the road he'd been traveling in the opposite direction. Even now, as he stared at her in the mirror, she caught no flicker of either sexual or romantic interest in his grim expression. His next words confirmed the fact.

"I'd better shave in bed," he said. "I can't stand on one leg as long as I thought."

5

MORE THAN ANYTHING, Brenna wanted to help Trip shave. But she knew her help wasn't what he most needed, knew his need was to go it alone, to prove to himself that he could do it.

"I'll finish breakfast," she said after she got his bed stand readied with mirror, waterbasin, towel, disposable razor.

With a heart as low as a sunken ship, Trip watched her leave his room. He knew he had to learn to do this with his left hand, yet he wanted Brenna's help. All she wanted, it was obvious, was to escape to the kitchen. And why wouldn't she, he reasoned harshly with himself.

Who'd want to be stuck on a holiday weekend in the middle of nowhere with an invalid? One who couldn't get out of bed or get back in unaided. One who couldn't wash his own back. One who had only barely brushed his teeth unaided. One who would surely need a blood transfusion after he shaved.

Some razzle-dazzle holiday this was for a relief vet who needed a steady paycheck badly enough to add "relief nurse" to her list of responsibilities. Nice work if you could get out of it.

"Oh, no!" Brenna gasped when she came in a little later with his breakfast tray. "Look at you. You're—why didn't you call for help?"

"Because a man's supposed to be able to shave his own face in the morning, that's why."

She set the tray down next to him on the bed. "You're bleeding all over the place, Trip. You can't—here, give me that." She held her hand out for the razor.

"No." He couldn't act as willing and eager as he felt, he knew. If she got even the slightest inkling he wanted her to patch up his botched job more than anything else in the world, she'd be asking for last week's pay and the fastest way back to San Jose.

"Okay. Have it your way." She picked up the tray. "No chow for you this morning. Byron and Malia just love sunny-side-up with salsa."

"You'd feed them my breakfast?"

"Care to watch?"

He held out the razor and suppressed a smile. "You win. But finish me up before my eggs get cold."

"In this heat, nothing's going to get cold." She put the tray back down and took the razor. Seated beside him, she dabbed at the spate of bloody spots on his face with the towel and began shaving where he'd missed. "I thought we signed an agreement last night on the issue of help when you need it."

"I only said I'd try."

"Don't talk. I'll nick you."

"Don't harangue me, then. I can't argue and stay still at the same time."

"Stick your chin out and shut up or you'll have two clefts in it instead of one." A cleft in his chin, a dimple waiting for a smile, a razor nick at the edge of his lower lip. His mouth so close she could press her own to it with a slight move forward. Brenna's fingers tightened on the razor handle. Careful.

Trip felt dizzy. A slight move forward and he could curl his arm around her, pull her into the kiss his lips hungered to place on hers. He closed his eyes, imagining her breasts crushed against his chest, her fingers wrapped around the back of his neck, the pressure of the headboard against his spine as she leaned into him and kissed him back.

"Ouch."

Brenna gasped and snatched the razor away, her eyes searching for fresh blood. "I'm sorry. . . did I nick you?"

"No." Trip opened his eyes, dazed. "Just. . . razor drag." It had felt so real, holding her in his mind like that. Each bruised vertebra of his upper spine hurt with the imagined memory of her weight against him.

"I'm sorry." She sighed. "I'm not much of a barber, I'm afraid."

"You're better than I am," he said quickly before she could put the razor down. "Don't leave me half-done."

Brenna reluctantly resumed her task. After a few moments of applied effort, she felt calm enough to comment, "My ex-husband, Fletcher, used to shave once in a blue moon with an ivory-handled straightedge his grand-uncle left him," she said. "He never could master the technique. Always came out with bits of toilet paper dotting his face like chicken pox. Another blue moon and he'd get the urge again and lose another round to the straightedge again."

"How long were you married?" Trip asked when she swished the razor in the basin.

"Four years. Long enough to learn how naive a twenty-year-old could be about love and marriage. He was my English professor in college."

"How did you end up with pet pigs instead of kids?"

"Fletch already had three children and a vasectomy from his second marriage. Byron and Malia were willed to me by the eccentric owner of a pair of llamas I once treated."

Trip had to wait until she swished again before he could inquire, "You were someone's third wife?"

Brenna nodded. "Naiveté, in my case, knew no bounds. I was also the third American Lit student he married. He had a weakness for coeds—whether he was married to one or not, it turned out. Maybe it was his name—Fletcher rhymes with lecher. He's well into his fifth student right now."

"Five. Good Lord."

"Hold still. I'm almost through." Holding her breath, she shaved the last patch of stubble from above his upper lip. Why was his mouth such a beautifully shaped temptation? "There, you're done and you've stopped bleeding. A quick rinse and breakfast is served."

With unnecessary haste, Brenna administered the final ablutions and set his breakfast tray on his lap.

"Mmm. Looks good." Trip had to suppress a note of disappointment in his voice at the contents of the tray. It held everything he'd ordered and nothing for Brenna, not even a cup of coffee to keep his own cup company. What had he expected, though? Wasn't it enough that he'd monopolized her every waking minute since he'd come home? Did she have to eat breakfast with him, too? "Have you already eaten?" he asked despite himself.

"No. I'm the just-coffee-until-noon type. Besides, I have to feed the pigs and the Dwarves, and then drive over to the Bender Ranch to check on Starbright's little bull."

Trip stared down at the tasty eggs staring back at him and instantly lost his appetite. *The Bender Ranch*. Never-married Dwight Bender had two strong arms, two long legs and a sweep-'em-up-with-no-argument reputation with women. Until that very moment, Trip had never given those facts a moment's thought. He'd merely rolled his eyes whenever Lita had observed aloud that Dwight was the *second* most eligible bachelor in the county, after Trip.

"Something wrong with the eggs?"

"Huh?" He looked up from them at Brenna. Dwight, he was certain, would be waiting with bated breath for this lovely woman's return to his ranch. How well had the two of them gotten to know each other out there in his cozy barn while she birthed that bull?

"You did say sunny-side up, didn't you?"

"Uh, no...I mean, yes..." His eyes dropped from hers to her yellow tube top. "I, uh, you're not wearing that out there, are you?" he blurted.

"Why—no, but—" Brenna looked down at herself and back up at him, speechless at his audacity.

"Sorry," he said quickly. "I didn't mean you don't look good. You do. What I meant was..." He attacked his eggs with his fork and mumbled, "Dwight Bender's not one to think saintly thoughts about a vet like you dressed in clothes like that."

She flushed and felt the color flood down her bare shoulders, right into her top. "Thanks for the tip, but Lita warned me about Dwight before I went out there."

"Oh? Did he live up to his reputation?" Trip didn't dare look up from the great interest he was pretending to have developed in his glass of grapefruit juice.

"Infinitely better than you've lived up to yours," Brenna replied, her tone twice as tart as the juice on Trip's tongue.

Trip sputtered and frowned at her over the rim of his glass. "Mine? *I'm* no smooth-talking fast mover."

"I know. Lita mentioned that, too." She went to the doorway and paused there to add before walking out, "I meant your reputation as one of the bravest, kindest human beings in this neck of the woods—or so your clients tell me."

She left Trip wordlessly lowering his glass to his tray. He listened to the slap-slap of Brenna's thong sandals across the hall floor. Brave. Kind. He heard her slamming drawers in her room. Changing clothes, no doubt, as she had probably intended to do all along. Listening, thinking, he ate the eggs she had fried to sunny perfection, sipped the coffee she had brewed thick and dark the way he liked it.

"I'll be back in an hour or so," she said, breezing past his door in jeans and a baggy T-shirt before he could swallow his last mouthful of eggs and call her back to apologize for each growl and scowl he'd had ample opportunity to both recall and regret while she changed.

He heard the slam of the back screen door and the lilting sound of her voice calling the Dwarves to breakfast.

"Let them in," he yelled, hoping she'd hear him through his open window.

He waited. No answer. No Dwarves. Only the sound of her car starting and the crunch of tires on the gravel driveway as Brenna set off for Bender's. Brave? Sometimes. Kind? Often enough. And useless. No question of that.

"Brave, kind and one fabulous hunk," Brenna muttered to herself on the rutted road to the Bender Ranch. Now she wondered if she shouldn't have included that third observation in her little speech in Trip's doorway. More than one of Trip's female clients had already said the same of him without any hesitation. Now, having met the object of their admiration, Brenna could clearly see why.

Even Dwight's ninety-five-year-old grandmother had once observed, with a wink at Brenna, "Seventy years ago I'd have let a man like Trip Hart park his boots under my bed anytime he liked."

Would she have let him park his crutch there, though, Brenna found herself wondering. And as she did, the sudden thought came to her of Trip wondering the same thing. Not about Violet Bender, of course, but about . . . well, about any woman he might want to . . .

Was he fearing that he'd never . . . that no woman would ever . . . ? Her fingers curled tighter around the steering wheel. She turned into Dwight Bender's dirt driveway and saw dust churn behind her in the rearview mirror. *If that's what Trip's thinking, he can think again. Why, he could park his crutch under my—*

Before she could complete the thought, she saw Dwight waiting for her, leaning against the side of his shiny red 4 × 4 pickup truck. He was blond, green eyed, bare to the waist, dressed only in snug, faded jeans that left little to the imagination. He didn't measure up to Trip, though. Brenna lifted her chin and got out of the car, knowing that whatever Dwight was thinking, he too could think again.

"How's Starbright?" she asked briskly.

"How are *you*?" Dwight countered.

"Sweltering, like you," she said with an impassive glance at his glistening chest. "You're getting sunburned."

He grinned and folded his arms over his sunburn. "And you're staying just as cool and frosty as you were yesterday."

"Once an iceberg, always an iceberg, Dwight. How's the new arrival?"

"He's coughing this morning." He steered her toward the barn, his hand on her right elbow. "You could always melt a little if you got the notion. . . ."

"Hmm. Maybe he's picked up a respiratory virus. Any nasal discharge?" She slipped out of his grasp and switched her vet bag to her right hand.

"Yep." He hitched his thumbs in his pants pockets. "How about thawing out just enough to have dinner with me tonight?"

"Thank you, but I have a dinner guest tonight."

"Whoa." Dwight blinked and took a step back. "Who aced me out before I even got to first base?"

"My boss," she coolly replied, and continued into the barn.

SPRAWLED IN HIS BED, Brenna's boss lay staring at a *Sports Illustrated* swimsuit issue, immune to each inch of bare female flesh in it. His thoughts were of Brenna's smile—and every other fascinating feature of her anatomy. He clenched his one good hand into a fist at the thought of Dwight watching her tend to that baby bull. Trip knew Dwight. Knew him, hell. He and Dwight had been bosom buddies from boyhood, and were to this day.

Trip knew his best friend, no question. The Dwight he knew would be walking his eyes all over Brenna right now. And his hands, too, given permission. He was probably roping her into going out with him tonight in that red-hot truck of his, angling for permission.

Trip threw the magazine aside and reached for his crutch. If Brenna was going joyriding with Romeo tonight, she wouldn't be around to cook dinner. If he couldn't have Brenna, Trip decided, he might as well defrost one of the steaks in the deep freeze. A thick, juicy one. Small comfort compared to succulent Brenna.

He pulled himself up very slowly out of the bed. There had to be a way to do this without her. Though he had to admit that doing it with her now seemed almost worth the embarrassment. He had barely maneuvered upright before his good leg shimmied beneath him and almost buckled at the knee. He clung to his crutch, swaying, praying for his swimming head to clear. Huge droplets of sweat rolled down his bare arm and torso. Suddenly his own kitchen seemed halfway around the world, a journey no fool would undertake. He gritted his teeth and took a wavering step, then another.

A distance that had never taken him more than a few seconds to travel with two good legs took twenty minutes to navigate once his head cleared and the shimmy stopped. He was drenched with sweat when he lurched into the kitchen and found two steaks defrosting on the counter. He swayed, staring at them. Now what?

Within seconds the scrunch of tires on gravel rendered the question moot.

Clutching two brown grocery bags to her chest, Brenna elbowed the screen door open and stopped partway in to gasp at the sight of Trip easing down into an oak ladder-back chair alongside the kitchen table. His unyielding leg cast made it impossible for him to sit properly, so he only half sat on one hip with his good arm on the table for a counterbalance.

"How did you—?"

"I did it," he cut in tersely. "That's all that matters."

Brenna walked in with her load and slid the bags onto the table. "You're soaking wet," she finally observed, after a long look at Trip told her how great a cost his effort had been to him.

He nodded. "It must be ninety in the shade today. What's in the bags?"

She rounded the table. "You're supposed to be in bed."

"Smells like peaches."

"You could have passed out."

"I miss the Dwarves. I got up to let them in."

"Trip, I said I wouldn't be long when I left."

"You took long enough," he said. "Picking peaches with Dwight in his orchard, from the smell of it."

"They were already picked. He insisted on giving them to me." She crossed the kitchen to the refrigerator, relishing the blast of icy air when she opened the door.

"That can't be all he insisted on."

"No, he wanted me to take more. I told him two sacks were plenty."

"I'm not talking peaches." Trip hated himself for fishing, but he had to know. "I'm talking Dwight, the smooth-talking fast mover."

"Oh. Him. Well, he did try to insist on taking me out to dinner tonight, but I said I was dining with you." She glanced over her shoulder at him, trying to detect from his expression whether she had heard or imagined a note of jealousy in his voice. "I am, aren't I?" she inquired, unable to detect a thing. "Or are you busy tonight?"

"Busy," he snorted. "Any blind man can see I'm going nowhere at a snail's pace." *Dining with you.* Small comfort if she was doing it out of some warped sense of duty, but comfort nonetheless if it kept Dwight out of the picture.

Brenna studied the contents of the refrigerator, wishing she didn't feel about Trip as she did, and further wishing the sight of him in white briefs didn't make the impression on her that it did. But it did. Her internal temperature was 100 degrees and rising. Ridiculous when she considered that most men's swimsuits were skimpier and tighter than Trip's briefs, yet no swimsuit on a beach had ever upped her libido to this level.

"I do believe I'll have a beer," she decided, and pulled one out of the fridge.

"Shine a tall, cool one my way, while you're at it." Trip sighed.

She raised an eyebrow and tapped the rim of the can possessively against her chest. "You're not getting a tall, cool anything until you're back in bed where you belong." *Out of sight under the sheet.* "Rest, rest and more rest. Dr. Jamison's orders. Remember?"

"I'll shine one my own way, then," he retorted, reaching for his crutch.

Brenna saw the heat flash of defiance in his dark eyes and brightened at the words he'd just spoken with such conviction. She hated to think of just how he had negotiated the distance from bed to kitchen, but she knew it had been his first giant step on the road to recovery. The last thing he needed at this crucial point was her helping hand.

"It's *your* funeral," she said, and walked out the back door with her beer. "I'll round up the Dwarves for you."

Instead of immediately calling the cats, she strolled with her beer to the edge of the back lawn, pondering the question of how Trip intended to get a can of brew from the refrigerator to either the kitchen table or his bed.

It took Trip only a moment of thought before he figured it out. Using his teeth and his able hand, he bound the unopened can snug to his arm cast with a kitchen towel. Flushed with triumph, he made the agonizing trip back to his bed and yelled out to Brenna for help.

Preceded by seven sleek calico cats, Brenna entered his room and found him back under the sheet, holding up his opened beer like the trophy it was.

"Thanks for nothing," he said with a half grin of forgiveness when she touched the rim of her can to his in a silent toast. They drank, their gazes locked during the instant that passed before the cats piled up onto the bed to greet their master with a chorus of excited meows.

"It's good to be home." Trip's blissful smile gave way to a tight grimace when the heaviest of the Dwarves leaped onto his bruised ribs.

Brenna gently shooed the calico back onto the mattress and then settled on the edge of the bed to join Trip in petting the meowing crowd. The cats were a warm mass of rippling movement, and somewhere in that sinuous sea of fur Brenna felt the slow brush of Trip's hand against hers. She sucked in a breath at his touch and then another when their flesh made contact again. In her right hand she still held her beer can. Her fingers tightened around the chilled aluminum cylinder as a lingering stroke, which she very deliberately initiated, made breathing an effort.

Trip, who had been murmuring soothing sounds as he petted the cats, fell as silent as she. The cats wound under and over and around their hands, and when Trip's hand came to curl around Brenna's, neither knew quite what to do next.

It took a discreet cough from the entrance to the room to break the connection, as well as the impasse. Brenna twisted around to find bright-eyed Byron and Malia in the open doorway, waiting to be invited in. Ears pricked forward, the two tiny pigs wiggled all over with the excitement and anticipation of joining the love feast on the bed.

"Well, don't just stand there wagging your little pig-tails and clearing your throats," Brenna said, motioning them in. "Come and see Trip."

They trotted in and Brenna lifted them onto the bed where, after three of the cats dispersed, they both joyfully toppled over on their backs to have their tummies rubbed.

Trip, a delighted smile on his lips, gave each pig's tummy equal attention and then looked up at Brenna. "Their bristles are so soft," he marveled, stroking his fingertips over Byron's shiny, solid black coat.

"Mmm," Brenna agreed, scratching one of the cats behind the ears, "just like an artist's paintbrush."

Byron sighed a sigh of sheer bliss and Trip chuckled. "What a gas. Minipigs. What breed did you say they are?"

"Chinese Potbelly Miniatures."

He shook his head. "Never heard of them."

"I hadn't, either, before I met these two. They're imported mostly out of Vietnam and they're still quite rare in this country."

"Expensive?"

Brenna grinned. "You're looking at over five thousand dollars' worth of expensive right here on your bed."

Trip blew out a low, appreciative whistle. "That was some satisfied client you had. Pricey gift."

"I saved his even pricier llamas before he died of cancer." Brenna shrugged. "I had no idea I was written into his will as the first in line to adopt his pigs. But I'm glad I was." She smiled fondly at Byron and tickled Malia's tender snout until it twitched. "I'm so madly in love with these two that I can't imagine life without them."

Trip watched the soft smile play on Brenna's lips and thought about how it might feel to be loved that much by her. And to love her that much in return. Madly in love. He was beginning to think he was halfway there where Brenna Deveney was concerned. His gaze lingered on her lips and then lowered to where her fingers caressed gentle circles on Malia's tiny little chest. Ah, to be that fortunate pig at this very moment, a willing recipient of Brenna's magic touch.

Trip cleared his throat. "How old are they? What do they eat?" A nice dry statistic or two should bring his suddenly high-flying imagination back to earth. "What's the story?"

"Byron's five and Malia's three," Brenna obliged. "They were born in Pescadero at Kiyoko Hansen's breeding farm. Kiyoko has even written a children's book about Chinese Potbellies. They love fruit and vegetables—and frozen juice bars. Byron's neutered and weighs about forty-five pounds, Malia weighs thirty-seven. He likes the Beatles, she likes Elton John. They're smart enough to open sliding glass doors and refrigerators, as well as roll over and play dead or sit up and beg. Malia can pirouette like a ballerina and Byron can leap like Baryshnikov. They don't shed hair or get fleas. *And* they're housebroken."

"You left out how affectionate and adorable they are," Trip added with an amused chuckle. "I think I'm in love."

Me, too. With you. "I also left out that they're learning Spanish from Lita." She cocked a teasing eyebrow at Trip. "And as you already know, they play a mean game of hide-and-seek."

"Yeah. They really knocked me for a loop in the middle of the last one."

They both laughed, and as their laughter died away into a comfy silence, Brenna mused that the day had suddenly become one of her best at the Hart Ranch. Here were two animal lovers on a bed with three cats who were absorbed in cleaning, preening or napping, and a pair of miniature pigs flat on their backs in a contented reverie all their own.

"This," declared Trip in a low, dulcet tone, "is the best day I've had since . . ." He glanced down at his arm cast and up at Brenna. "Thanks for everything you've done—and haven't done."

She reached out and touched his hand where it rested on Byron's chest. "I'm glad you're feeling better. How's your head?"

"Great." *It only spins into outer space every time you touch me. Keep touching.*

Trip closed his eyes, willing his hand to lie still under hers. Her touch was heaven, but had been extended only out of sympathy, he was sure. If he didn't steel himself, he'd glide his hand right up her bare arm and pull her toward him on the bed until her mouth met his or her breasts pressed softly into his chest—or both. Accepting her sympathetic touch was one thing but doing the other would invite certain rejection.

As if she had read his mind, she slid her hand away and reached for her beer on the nightstand. Trip opened his eyes, reached for his own can and breathed a mental sigh of relief at having preserved himself from either blushing under the sheet or grabbing her against her will.

Brenna drank deep, wondering how to escape the room with her pride intact after being so politely but firmly rejected. She wondered, with even greater consternation, how she had mistaken that earlier tactile contact for the deliberate caress it had apparently not been. His hand under hers a moment ago had been as stiff and unresponsive as the oak headboard of his bed. A grave mistake to reach out like that and get cut to the quick. A mistake she wouldn't make again, under any circumstance.

She stood. "Are ham sandwiches okay for lunch?"

"I'll bite."

"Pickles?"

"Lots."

"Sweet or dill?"

"Sweet." *Like you.* "Uh, why don't we eat outside under the old blue oak where it's shady. I can lie on the chaise from the patio if you'll move it for me."

"Aren't you exhausted from this morning?"

"Yes, as a matter of fact. But I can't stand being cooped up all day. It's like an oven in here."

"I know, but—"

"If you help me out, it won't take half the energy I burned up this morning."

She pursed her lips and frowned while her heart leaped up at the offhand permission she had just received to touch him. "Okay," she said with a shrug of pretended neutrality. "I'll come back and help you after I get things ready."

Not one of the napping cats or either of the two snoring pigs took the slightest note of her exit. Only Trip. He watched Brenna's long, jean-clad legs and rounded bottom as she left the room—and prayed that she'd change back into shorts before lunch. There was no law against looking, thank heaven.

While Trip prayed, Brenna put on her shorts and tube top and went out to drag the chaise from the flagstone patio to the shade of the oak. A slight breeze had picked up. Nice. Maybe a little fresh air would do Trip some good. If nothing else, she'd feel far more comfortable serving him lunch in the great outdoors than in his bedroom, she decided. Especially since the vacant side of his bed had become the imagined scene of her every soft-core fantasy about him. She flushed, remembering how very nearly her fantasies had provoked her into throwing herself at him just moments ago.

When everything was ready outside, sandwiches and iced tea made, the webbed patio chaise padded with a thick quilt and pillows, Brenna went to get Trip.

He was half-upright on the edge of the mattress, ready to swing his leg cast over the side when she came in.

"Watch," he said, a nugget of pride in his voice. "I've almost got this move wired." With a heavy grunt, he hauled over from the waist and hip and eased the cast down the steep angle from the bed to the floor. "There." He panted. "I didn't even wake up the cats or pigs. Now, if I prop up on my good elbow and push up and use my other leg like this . . ." He grunted, pushed and came into a position that would allow him to rise from the bed, using his crutch as a support. "Ta-da," he exulted as he came up triumphant on his one able foot.

Brenna enthusiastically applauded his effort. "Way to go, Doc."

"And now, if my nurse will simply step under my big white wing here—" he held his arm cast up and out for her to fit her bare shoulder to the crook of his armpit "—we'll stroll outside."

Permission to touch, Brenna reminded herself, and slid her left arm around his back at the waist. For balance, she placed her right palm flat in the middle of his abdomen just below his bruised rib cage. She glanced over at Byron and Malia and saw their ears twitch.

"Stay," she commanded, and they did. So did the napping cats.

"This is a lot easier with help." Trip panted softly as they limped together out of the room. When they were halfway down the hall, he stopped to rest and Brenna pulled a towel from the hall bath to wipe the perspiration from his face and torso.

"Trip," she said, "maybe this isn't such a good idea. If you pass out, I can't get you back into bed by myself."

"I'm not going to pass out."

She pressed the towel to the damp, dark red hair on his chest, feeling fairly light-headed herself at standing so close to this beautiful man.

"Once I'm outside on that chaise, my pulse will go down and I'll stop sweating like a pig."

"Pigs don't have sweat glands," she corrected, draping the towel over her shoulder and fitting herself to his side again.

"Right. I forgot. The basic difference between man and pig. Pigs are cleaner."

He chuckled at that and Brenna joined in. They started off again. For himself, Trip cared not a whit how long it took to reach the chaise. The longer the better, from his vantage point. After all, here he was, enjoying the soft press of Brenna's bountiful left breast against his right side, the feel of her cool palm flat on his midsection. Her fragrant, silky hair swung back and forth, brushing his shoulder as she moved with him. Life wasn't always this sweet, even for an able-bodied man.

Brenna too was thinking how very right they felt together. Even in this awkward position, her body somehow fit naturally to Trip's, except where her breast was crushed to his side. Could he feel how perfectly they fit from thigh to hip to waist? She imagined standing front to front with him, could almost feel the silky brush of his chest hair on the tips of her breasts.

Moving as one, they finally made it to the chaise, where Brenna helped Trip settle into it and breathed her own huge sigh of relief at the same moment he breathed his.

"I don't know about you, but I'm starved," Trip said.

"Me, too. Catch your breath while I get the food." It was her own breath that needed to be caught, and fetching lunch back and forth from the kitchen to the oak tree in the heat of the day was no help.

Trip wolfed down one sandwich in a matter of seconds, then launched into a second one with a small moan of appreciation. "You know," he said, holding up his sandwich and appraising it as if it were a rare jewel, "if you had been cooking my meals in the hospital, I might never have left." *And if you had been my nurse, wild horses couldn't have dragged me into that taxi even one day early.*

"I'll remind you of that after I ruin the steaks on the barbecue tonight," Brenna replied with a wry smile. "I'm a disaster at steak."

"So was Suzanne," Trip said after a moment. His voice softened with remembrance. "I always grilled the steaks when we were married. She was a disaster at sandwiches, too, and everything else in the kitchen." He took another bite of sandwich. "These are great."

Brenna couldn't help feeling inordinately pleased at Trip's praise and dismayed by what sounded like a note of longing in his voice for his ex-wife. Was he still carrying a torch for her? That might explain his lack of interest in dating, much less remarrying.

"It's not as if I slaved over a hot stove half the morning," she demurred.

"Maybe not," he granted, "but Suzanne never slaved over a hot stove for even a half minute. Her head was too high up in the clouds for—" He halted and shot a glance

Discover Masquerade

WITH TWO FREE BOOKS

Masquerade historical romances bring the past alive with splendour, excitement and romance. As a special introductory offer we will send you two Masquerade romances together with a cuddly Teddy Bear and a Mystery Gift - completely FREE.

We will also reserve a subscription for you which means you could go on to enjoy four exciting books published every two months, delivered to your door before they're available in the shops for just £1.99 each - postage and packing FREE. Plus a FREE Newsletter giving you information on the top authors, competitions, (our last lucky reader won a microwave oven), and much more.

What's more there are no strings attached, you can stop receiving books at any time, so don't delay, complete and return this card NOW!

Complete the coupon overleaf.

FREE BOOKS COUPON

Fill in the coupon now!

Yes! Please send me two FREE Masquerade romances together with my FREE Teddy and Mystery Gift and reserve a subscription for me. If I decide not to subscribe I shall write to you within 10 days. The FREE books and gifts are mine to keep in any case. I understand that I can cancel or suspend my subscription at any time simply by writing to you.

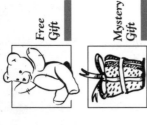

Free Gift

Mystery Gift

Name _____ SA1M

Address _____

_____ Postcode _____

Signature _____
(I am over 18 years age.)

Send no money now - take no risks

Reader Service
FREEPOST
P.O. Box 236
Croydon
Surrey
CR9 9EL

NO STAMP NEEDED

The right is reserved to refuse an application and change the terms of this offer. Offer expires Dec 31st 1991. You may be mailed with other offers from Mills and Boon and other reputable companies as a result of this application. Readers in Southern Africa, write to: Independent Book Services Pty. Postbag X3010. Ranburg 2125 South Africa. Overseas & Eire - send for details.

at Brenna. "How much has Mom bent your ear about me and Suzanne?"

Brenna shrugged and swirled the ice in her tall tea glass. "Not much. She said that Suzanne fell in with a group—a new-age spiritual commune—that was leasing a ranch near here. I know she divorced you after she fell in love with the leader of the group. Lita says they moved the commune north of San Francisco after the rancher here refused to renew the lease."

"You know about Aura, my daughter?"

Brenna nodded. "I know Suzanne has primary custody and that Aura was going to spend July and August here with you."

"Yeah, she sure was." He rapped a knuckle dispiritedly against his leg cast. "Until *this* happened to postpone it." He rapped his knuckle again, harder. "I was going to take her to Disneyland while she was here. And camping and fishing, too. Some fun I'm going to be now for a six-year-old when she *does* get out here."

"Lita says Aura loves the ranch. Kids are flexible," Brenna assured him. "At least Fletcher's kids were, what little I saw of them."

"When they're your own, it's different," Trip insisted. "And when you see them only a few times in a year, you want each visit to be special and memorable."

Brenna brushed crumbs off her lap. "Well, I can tell you one thing. Aura will never forget Pygmalia and Lard Byron once she lays eyes on them."

"Only if they're still here when I'm well enough for her to visit," Trip said darkly.

Brenna saw his lower lip curl with the downturn his mood had taken from the moment he'd spoken his ex-wife's name. "Why wouldn't they still be here?"

He stared at her in disbelief that she could even ask. "Because once my practice is sold, you'll be looking for another job."

"Sold!"

"What else?" He glanced at his arm cast. "I can't even feel my right hand, much less flex it. Surgery is one thing no one can do with one hand tied behind his back. Hell, I can't even deliver a calf with one hand. And I'm sure as hell not going to be able to stand on my own two feet to do it. What would you do in my shoes?"

"If I had your practice, I'd hold on to it for dear life until I was positive I had to sell," Brenna stated firmly.

Trip snorted, his eyes fierce and dark and hopeless as he looked up at her. "Still betting that therapy's going to make me good as new?"

"Want to bet it isn't?"

"Sure. Five hundred bucks? A thousand?"

"Don't be insane. I can't lay a bet like that with what I earn doing relief work."

"You can if you're sure you're going to win it."

"No one can be that sure of anything in this world," she said, meeting his unwavering gaze.

"Now why doesn't that sound like the same Pollyanna who gave me that ounce-of-hope routine last night? Who pulled the rug out from under you, besides Fletcher the Lecher?"

After a moment of uncertainty, she replied, "My ex-prospective clinic partners in San Jose. One day I had a partnership in the bag and the next day I didn't." She stood to gather up empty plates and glasses, reluctant to say more.

"What happened?"

"We had a disagreement about—" she hesitated and bit her lip. "I was too progressive for their conservative tastes, it turned out. That was that. And here I am."

"Sorry I can't give you a hand with all this," said Trip, adding his glass to hers on top of a plate.

"You can give me one in a minute," she promised, heading into the kitchen and away from the subject of her lost partnership.

"How?" he called after her.

"It's a surprise," she called back.

"Give me a hint."

"Smooth and creamy."

Smooth and creamy. *Hola.* He lolled his head back and closed his eyes, letting the bud of her hint blossom forth in his mind. The only smooth and creamy substance she could possibly need his hand for was sun lotion. On her back. Ah, yes. He imagined the warmth of her skin under his palm, the curve of her neck, the cream-smooth lotion, his fingertips slowly massaging it in vertebra by vertebra. . . .

He had progressed down to the base of Brenna's spine in his imagination before he heard her soft footstep on the grass, felt her even softer touch on his shoulder.

"Trip?"

"Hmm?"

"Wake up. You've got a job on your hand."

Trip smiled, kept his eyes closed and held out his hand for the sun lotion.

6

WHEN HIS HAND REMAINED empty of sun lotion, Trip opened his eyes. His heart slumped at the sight of Brenna hefting a small crank-type ice-cream freezer onto the patio table next to his chaise.

"It's peach," she told him. "We can take turns cranking."

"Peachy." He snatched his outstretched hand back and settled it on his bare stomach where he drummed his fingers in agitation. Smooth and creamy. Not quite what he'd had in mind.

Brenna tried to keep her eyes off those rhythmic fingers of his and the taut skin they drummed. What, now, had she done to irritate him? Was he the Chocolate Fudge type? *Peachy*. The tone in which he'd said it left a lot to be desired.

"You crank first," she said, "while I fill the pool."

"What pool?"

"The plastic wading pool. For Byron and Malia. It's over on the north side of the house. The water needed changing, so I emptied it this morning. They like a wallow when it's hot, though, so I'd better refill it." She took a step back. "Go ahead and start. I'll be back in a—"

"Could you move it over here without a lot of trouble?" Trip cut in. "I'd like to watch those two wallow."

"Of course. They love an audience."

"You look like you could use a swim, yourself."

If he meant she looked hot and bothered, she thought, he was right. "I join them whenever I can. They like company even better than an audience."

"Have a dip, then. Leave the ice cream to me."

"Okay. I'll take over if you get tired." Mentally fanning herself with every step, she went to get the pool.

Trip gave the freezer an affectionate pat on its wooden side. Ask the right question at the right moment and things could zing from down to up in a split second. He could see it now. Brenna in a bikini, frolicking with Byron and Malia in the kiddie pool. No hospital could ever have offered that to its captive patients on the Fourth of July.

Brenna settled the kiddie pool in the shade just a few feet from Trip's chaise. It was baby-blue plastic, two feet deep and decorated with cartoon characters. She set the nozzle end of the garden hose in it and turned the water on all the way.

"There." She wiped her hands on her white shorts and watched Trip crank for a moment. "How's it going?"

"Peachy." In fact, his ribs ached on every downturn, but he grinned up at her. "When Jamison comes out on Tuesday, we can tell him I started physical therapy without him."

"Just take it slow and don't overdo," Brenna warned, though the flexing bulge of Trip's biceps made that possibility seem more than remote. She caught a breath, seeing the muscles in his forearm ripple and smooth . . . ripple and smooth . . . with each rotation of his arm. She had an image of that strong arm curling around her waist and holding her against him.

"Have you seen me overdo anything since I got back?" he chided, and allowed his eyes a covert tour of Brenna's body from her bare toes to her sherry-rich eyes where he stopped and raised his eyebrows in punctuation to his question.

She swallowed and took a step back. "No." Several steps back. "I'd—uh, better go and get the pigs—and change into a swimsuit."

Do that. Make my day. "Would you bring my sunglasses?" he called after her. "They're in my nightstand drawer."

After changing in her room, Brenna frowned at her reflection in the full-length mirror and wished she had brought her black bikini instead of her red tank swimsuit. A bikini might prod Trip to give her a second look and like what he saw. Not that he hadn't taken notice of her shorts and tube top earlier. In the wrong way. Still, it was understandable that he'd object to his relief vet making house—or ranch—calls strapless and in shorts. Oh, well. She swiped a tube of sunscreen off her dresser, threw a beach towel over her shoulder and went to rouse the pigs.

They were still on their backs, snoring, on Trip's bed. "Time for a swim," she said, at which they rolled over in unison, hopped off the bed and scrambled down the hall. She followed them and then remembered Trip's sunglasses.

They were, as he'd said, in his nightstand drawer. In the opposite front corner of the drawer was an unopened box of condoms. Brenna sat down on the bed with his glasses in one hand and picked up the box. It was sealed. The expiration date on the bottom had passed two months ago. How long had they been there, unopened, unused? She put the box back, thinking.

An image rose in her mind of Trip's fingers breaking that seal, of her own fingers sheathing him in that protection. Then slowly, as if it contained a volatile explosive, she slid the drawer shut.

The image persisted, though, even after she'd handed Trip his glasses and put Byron and Malia into the partly filled pool, where they snorted and splashed and squealed in glee when she squirted them with the hose.

Sweet heaven. Had he envisioned a bikini? Trip couldn't recall. All he could think now was second-skin red. Safe from detection behind his mirrored sunglasses, he feasted his eyes on the deep cleavage between Brenna's breasts and the snug twin curves of her bottom while she circled the outside perimeter of the pool, teasing the pigs with bursts from the hose nozzle.

Brenna dropped the jetting hose back into the pool and stepped in. She lowered herself into the shallow water. "Ohhhh. It's like ice." She scooped water up over her shoulders and shivered with a childlike giggle of delight.

The revolving motion of Trip's arm and hand slowed to a stop, just as it had moments earlier when Brenna walked out, a goddess in red. Now, shielded behind his glasses, he focused on the tight twin points of her nipples where they hardened against wet red nylon. He circled his lips with his tongue.

Careful, man, or you'll be blushing like a virgin. He breathed deep and switched his attention to Byron, who was nosing the hose end from the bottom of the pool. Up the nozzle surged, like a wild thing spouting full blast, and thoroughly doused Trip on the chaise.

"Byron! Trip! Oh, no!" Brenna flung the hose away, lunged out of the pool and grabbed her towel. "Oh . . . you're drenched." She whisked Trip's glasses off and wiped his streaming face.

Trip gasped, stunned almost breathless both by the icy shock of his surprise shower and his suddenly eye-boggling proximity to the female curves he'd only moments ago admired from afar. As if in answer to his prayers, Brenna was bending over him. The shiny-wet upper hemispheres of her breasts rounded out over the scooped top of her suit.

"I'm sorry about this . . . he loves the nozzle. . . ." She wiped Trip's neck and throat, dripping her own wetness all over him as she mopped. "He's such a clown at times. . . ." Her motions slowed when she came to Trip's chest. She rubbed the towel over his flat brown nipples and saw them pucker into hard dots from the friction. Feeling the starch go out of her legs, she eased down onto one knee next to the chaise.

Leaves fluttered overhead in the hot breeze, dappling the shade and everything in it with dancing puddles of light. Her motions slowed. She dried his arm cast and pressed the towel to his bruised ribs.

"Tell me if it hurts."

"I've hurt worse."

"I knew I should have left the pool and the hose where they were. This was a crazy idea."

"Hey, that's *my* idea you're calling crazy," he retorted softly.

"I'm the one who let you talk me into it," she murmured, skipping the towel past his water-logged briefs to his legs.

"It could have been worse. I could have been fully dressed."

"It's bad enough as it is. Look at you." She dabbed at his dripping plaster cast. "You're soaked."

"So are you."

"That was the idea. Not this." She dragged the damp towel down his able leg, unable to stop thinking of the area where it joined his body.

"I'll survive." Trip was exerting the same effort in staring up into the branches of the oak tree instead of into Brenna's scooped neckline. When she finished, he vowed, he'd get back behind his sunglasses fast—if he didn't embarrass himself first.

As if she'd read his mind, Brenna finished with his leg and dropped the towel in a heap into his lap.

"I'll finish this," she announced, turning to the freezer with what Trip could only translate as a sigh of relief. Hearing it, he shot a reproachful glance at Byron. *Thanks, bud, for making me twice the chore I was a few minutes ago.*

Up to his nostrils in water, Byron blew out a bubbly sigh of contentment in return.

"Let me," Trip said, and reached for the lever where his hand closed over Brenna's.

"No." She tightened her grip. "I've already gotten you in one fix today. I'm not going to have your doctor giving me the third degree about how you got heat exhaustion when you were supposed to have been resting."

Trip curled his fingers around her wrist. "Don't worry about that. I'll answer to Jamison."

"Trip—"

"Let go and let me do something around here besides being a burden to you."

Brenna sat back on her heels and looked at him. His fingers pressed into the soft flesh of her wrist. She wondered if he could feel her pulse race into high gear at his touch. She herself could feel it in the rapid thud of her heart.

"You're not a burden, Trip." Her fingers were glued to the lever. She was loath to release it if it meant he'd stop touching her. "I'm a doctor...like you. Whether it's people or animals, I like taking care of them. Don't you?"

"Sure, I do—but taking care of a guy and being stuck with him are two different things."

"What if I don't feel 'stuck with him'?"

"What if you do and you're just too polite to complain?"

"I don't. And I'm not," she added with greater emphasis. "If I had a complaint, you'd know it. One thing I learned from my marriage was not to live with a thorn in my side."

"Even if the thorn is writing your paycheck?"

"Even then. Fletch put me through my first two years of vet school before he started coming home late or not at all. I could have stayed with him until I graduated, but I didn't. I divorced him and took out a loan to put myself through. Does that answer your question?"

Trip relaxed his grip on her and slid his hand back over hers. "Yes. And I'm sorry I was ass enough to ask it."

She turned her hand palm up under his in silent acceptance of his apology. "You're not used to really depending on anyone, are you?"

"Me? No. I've never felt so helpless—or useless—in my life." He glanced down at his hand in hers. "There's a prime example," he scoffed. "You're holding *my* hand when it should be the other way around."

"It can be the other way." She turned his hand over and carefully placed hers palm-down in it. "There. Now *you're* holding mine. And I don't feel at all helpless or useless in that position."

Trip's fingers very lightly curved over hers and stayed there. Brenna held her breath at this small miracle, his hand holding hers without sidling away after a wary moment of contact.

"Do you always humor your difficult patients like this, Dr. Deveney?" he asked with a strained smile.

"Always, Dr. Hart. They get better faster that way." Very lightly she squeezed his hand.

He squeezed back, the slightest of pressures, and the strain left his face. "Better faster, eh? Come to think of it, I do feel a lot better now than I did yesterday."

"You look a lot better, too," she assured him. "The dark circles under your eyes are gone. Did you sleep all right once you got settled?"

"Better than in the hospital where they wake you every thirty minutes for a bath or a shot or a pill or a pep talk. I'm glad I'm home."

She glanced over at the house. "So am I. It gets lonely out here after Lita leaves every afternoon. Of course, there are always the Dwarves and my two little water babies here." She nodded toward the kiddie pool. "But it's not the same as having someone else around. Especially when the coyotes howl after midnight."

Trip nodded. "I know. Everything seems bigger after dark. The ranch, the house, the bed—" He stopped, surprised, then chagrined that he'd actually voiced that last intimate detail. But Brenna was returning his gaze without the slightest expression of embarrassment, as if acknowledging that her bed, too, had a habit of widening into a vast dark wasteland every night. And her hand was still resting in his, indication enough that she hadn't taken what he'd just said as the blatant come-on it might have sounded like.

"Trip . . . could you move your leg over just a bit so I can sit?" she asked, unfolding as gracefully as she could from her cramped position on the lawn. "My knees are killing me."

"Oh. Sure." Trip crossed his leg over the one in the cast and pulled her by the hand to sit alongside and facing him. He chuckled when he saw her knees. "Don't look now, but you're sprouting grass."

She laughed, too, and plucked with one hand at the damp green blades embedded in her freckled knees. "Look at that. What if I'm scarred for life?"

"That's the price of humoring a guy, I guess." With the greatest nonchalance he'd ever pretended in his life, he led their still-twined hands to rest on the bare, freckled top of her thigh closest to him.

"You know, that ice cream won't be dessert until dinnertime at this rate," Brenna pointed out after giving up on her ravaged knees and riveting her attention back on the matter at hand—or *in* hand, to be specific.

"You'll have to arm-wrestle me for it," Trip murmured, tightening his hand around hers.

"Which wouldn't even be a contest since your arm is three times the size of mine?"

"Something like that."

"I won't even attempt it, then."

"Ah. You do know how to humor a man."

"What I'll do is just slide the bucket out of your reach and crank away."

"Uh-uh. You'd have to slide your hand out of mine, and I'm not letting go until we settle the issue of who's doing the chores here."

"Trip—" She tried to pull away and couldn't. His hand had become a vise, steely and inescapable around hers.

"I'm elected, Brenna." Gently, but implacably, he pulled her hand forward and held it captured in his against his chest.

Brenna stared into the heated darkness of his eyes, just inches from hers. "I paid for the cream and the sugar in that freezer container. And Dwight gave those peaches to me, not you. It's *my* recipe and I'll do what I please with it."

"Not when it's in *my* ice-cream freezer."

She leaned forward until she was almost nose to nose with him. "Let go."

"Not until we both see eye to eye on this."

"If you keep this up . . ." She moistened her lips. That dimple at the corner of his mouth. His tempting mouth. She was so close she could feel his breath on her lips.

"Give in and I'll let go."

"Trip . . ." His mouth was so inviting, but she couldn't close the scant inches between them and kiss it. Not against his will, as she was sure it would be if she did.

"Brenna . . ." Her lips were lush, parted, ready. If she moved a millimeter closer he'd do something he knew she wouldn't forgive.

She moved and he was done for, doing it, touching his mouth to hers. Her fist, enclosed in his, splayed flat against his chest. He felt it and steeled himself for the angry push to come. What came, though, was the twin press of her breasts against him, the twin press of her lips against his. Then came the shock of realization. She was kissing him back!

Brenna almost gasped with astonishment when he didn't draw back, when his lips moved on hers and then suddenly breathed her in as if he'd been waiting too long to merely taste her. His fingers, still flattened to his chest by her breasts, shifted and edged into her cleavage.

The first slip of his tongue into her mouth sent a shock wave of sensation pulsing through her. The second one sent her palms up to frame his cheeks and feel them hollow with each ever-deeper tongue-dive that she matched with a plunge of her own.

They came apart, gasping for breath, his fingers still curled into her top. Brenna dropped her hands from Trip's face to his chest. The hair there was silky, still damp from his surprise shower. Under her right palm she felt his heart beat in a rapid tattoo that vibrated through her hand, up her arm and into her body where her own heart drummed an erratic rhythm of its own.

"I—" He stared at his hand and wrenched his fingers out of the top of her suit as if her flesh had at that moment electrocuted him. "Sorry," he said, his voice shaky. He swallowed hard and repeated, "Sorry—I didn't mean to jump you like that. I—"

Brenna drew back. "Jump me? *I'm* the one who—" She stopped, startled into frustrated silence by the expression on his face. It was a mixture of remorse, regret and something more. In a flash, she realized it was shame. Shame over kissing her? "Trip—"

He held up his hand. "Don't say it. A little sexual harassment from the boss is the last thing you need here." He took a deep breath. "I'm sorry I crossed the line. It won't happen again."

"Trip, I crossed the line, too."

"You don't have to save my face for me," he muttered. "Even a cripple should get his face slapped if he deserves it."

"Cripple." Brenna pushed off from his chest and stood up. "You should slap your own face for calling yourself that."

"Spare me the hope routine, Pollyanna, as well as the lecture. I know what I did. I know what I am." Trip flung his forearm over his forehead and closed his eyes.

"So do I," Brenna snapped, and hauled the ice-cream freezer over to her chair where she started cranking. "What you are, Dr. Hart, is a world-class kisser who's probably a world-class lover, as well."

His eyes flew open at that, then dropped shut again. "I might have been once upon a time. But I'm not now."

It was his flash of surprise that gave her the courage to say, "I enjoyed what happened as much as you did, Trip. And I'm not saving your face or trying to build up your ego by saying it. I wanted that to happen. I've been wanting it for the last two weeks."

Trip snorted. "Tell me another. I only left the hospital yesterday, remember?"

"Who could forget? What *you* forget is that I've lived in your house all that time. I've looked through your photo albums with Lita. I know you better than I know some of my good friends. I've sat at your desk, worked your practice, dusted under your bed. I know you're loved and respected and admired in this community— and lusted after by a certain segment of the female population, as well."

"Lust no more, ladies." Trip sighed, after slitting his eyes open again at Brenna's final observation.

"Does that include me?" Brenna inquired, cranking furiously.

"What woman lusts after a cripple on a crutch?"

"Cripple, ha! There's more than one part of you that isn't out of order," Brenna accused, angered enough by his self-inflicted put-down to further inquire, "Or was that towel in your lap levitating all by itself?"

Trip's hand shot from his forehead to the towel. "I'm not . . ."

"You were."

"I—"

"I'm not blind. You were."

"Okay. I was. But only because I'm a man and not a—a block of ice."

"That's not what you were calling yourself a minute ago," she sagely pointed out.

"That's not the point. It's not every day I get that close to a 38C in a low-cut swimsuit," he growled, bunching the towel up so that nothing could show, one way or the other.

"Thanks for the compliment, but 36 is more like it. And I was the one who got close," Brenna corrected, noting that his eyes slid a hooded glance over at the inches in dispute as she bent forward and cranked.

He looked so vulnerable for an instant, so like a kid without a dime at a candy store, that her heart turned over. *Oh, Trip. Why can't you see you're attractive just as you are? You're sensitive and intelligent, broad chested and slim hipped and one hundred percent virile male, if only you'll look beyond your new limitations.*

The newness was the problem, though, she reasoned as Trip subsided into silence. He was still emotionally raw from what had happened to him. And he hadn't been aware until only a few minutes ago that she didn't find him repulsive. Even now, after she had openly admitted enjoying his kiss, he wouldn't let himself believe her. Why? For the same reason he wouldn't let himself harbor any hope for his future?

She glanced up at him. His eyes were closed again, his forearm flung over his forehead. Was he thinking that the less he hoped, the less disappointment he'd face in the long run? Brenna bit her lip and strained against the lever as the ice cream thickened. She reflected on her own disappointment at the clinic, and the weeks it had taken to accept the unchangeable.

Like Trip, she knew how bitterness could eat away until it hurt more than whatever had caused it. Like Trip, she faced an uncertain future. How many times had she despaired of ever being more than a salaried clinic vet building up someone else's practice? How many times had Trip despaired that he wouldn't be able to use his hand in surgery or even in general practice? Could she, of all people, blame him for refusing to hope against hope?

He could still love, though, she argued with herself. And be loved. And satisfy a woman, judging from his finesse with so evocative a caress as a kiss. Not that she expected him to fall as hard for her in two days as she had fallen in two weeks for *him*. But he was interested after only two days. Despite himself. Hugely interested, judging from his earlier response under the towel.

"Is it ice cream already?" Trip asked.

Brenna jumped, disoriented by the question, and found Trip's quizzical gaze fixed on her. It took a moment to realize that the deeper she had moved into thought, the slower she had cranked. Now the lever stood still in her slack hand, testament to the extent of her reverie. She came back to herself and pushed against considerable resistance. She added her other hand to the effort.

"It's getting there," she mumbled, flushing. How long had she sat there? Staring into space. Thinking about Trip. Thinking about *that*. Of all things. Right in front of the man. She flushed deeper, grateful that he couldn't possibly know what heights her thoughts had reached.

"Here." Trip held out a hand. "Bring it over here and no arguing. Even with only one arm, I'm stronger than you are with two."

Without a word she set the freezer back on the table beside him as he'd asked. He gave it a turn without half the effort she had expended. "Just a few more minutes," he said.

"I'll get bowls and spoons."

Brenna sped into the kitchen and spent several minutes staring into the cupboard, pressing her palms to her burning cheeks. She slid her hands down over the wet nylon of her suit. Her nipples were hard, and not from the cooling damp of the material against them. She smoothed her hands down to her lower abdomen. There, inside, she throbbed with a woman's need to make love, to touch and be touched, to surround a man and be filled with him. Not just any man, but a man she both wanted and loved. Trip. Except that however much he might want, he didn't yet love.

Brenna let her hands drop to her sides. She remembered making one-sided love to Fletcher once after he had taken his desire back to his classroom for a freshman coed. Sex in their marriage had never been that memorable, but she would never forget the dismal fizzle of that night or the emptiness she felt afterward. Sex without mutual love, she had learned then, and relearned after her divorce, was not better than no sex at all.

Trip knew it, too, she told herself. A man who took his pleasures at random wouldn't have a sealed box of condoms on the wrong end of its shelf life in his bedroom. A man who had sex without love might not even keep them in stock.

"Ice cream," she said out loud to steady herself and lower her sexual temperature. "The subject is bowls and spoons and ice cream and how to get through the rest of this fractured lunch."

They ate the creamy-smooth stuff in virtual silence in the shade of the old oak tree. Only the click of spoons in bowls could be heard, and an occasional watery gurgle from Byron and Malia basking in their pool.

Brenna finished first, barely a spoonful ahead of Trip. She patted her stomach and broke the silence. "That was superb, even if the bathroom scale says otherwise tomorrow morning."

"On you it won't show," Trip asserted, licking his spoon.

"Thank you, but after I make peach cobbler for dessert tonight it will."

He gave her a sideways glance. "If you're sticking around for dinner because of me, don't. Go out with Dwight if you want."

She shook her head. "I already thawed two steaks and—"

"I can eat the other one for lunch tomorrow," Trip cut in.

"*And*—as I was saying—I don't want to go out with Dwight."

"Why not?"

"Because I don't date smooth talkers or fast movers."

He shot her a quick glance and then stared into his ice cream. "Who *do* you date? If you don't mind my asking."

"No one."

"Come on," he prodded. "There must be someone back in San Jose taking cold showers until you come back."

Brenna shook her head. "There isn't. It's as simple as that. And now that we're on the subject, who do *you* date, Trip? If you don't mind *my* asking, that is."

"No one. I'm allergic to dating."

"So I hear. I only asked because I couldn't believe my ears."

"Who's been bending them?"

She shrugged. "No one in particular."

"My mother, I'll bet."

"She mentioned it in passing. So did Violet Bender."

"I'm not surprised," Trip said with a dry glance at her. "They've both been conspiring to marry Dwight and me off for years."

"Dwight didn't seem to be allergic to a date," Brenna ventured.

"Allergic? Dwight?" Trip almost laughed. "He's a master of the game. He has women eating out of his hand from one end of the county to the other. It's marriage he's allergic to."

"And you'd rather I joined Dwight's fan club instead of eating dinner with you?"

Trip's smile faded. "No. I wouldn't. I just didn't want you to feel obligated when you could be out on the town having fun. That's all."

"It would be easy enough, if I felt obligated, to call your mother and threaten to quit unless she came back to take care of you."

"Maybe you should."

Brenna blew out a sharp breath. "Why?"

He was silent for a long moment and then said, "Because no patient should be as hot for his nurse as I was for you a few minutes ago."

"Trip . . ." She hesitated, searching for words. "The attraction is mutual, okay? I didn't mean to throw myself at you, but it happened and I'm not sorry to learn you didn't mind." She blew out another frustrated breath. "Or maybe I am. It was easier when I thought you thought I was chopped liver."

"When I thought *you* thought *I* was the same thing, you mean," he said.

"Whatever. Now things are twice as awkward between us. We were better off keeping our distance."

Trip didn't reply to that. He just stirred his spoon around and around his empty bowl and followed the circular movement with brooding eyes.

Brenna felt permanently welded to her chair, unable to rise and pick her way through everything that was out in the open now between them, so to speak. Well, not everything. She wouldn't be ready for some time to tell him the full story of how her partnership had been lost because she reached out and touched and got burned by human suspicion and fear. Who knew what could happen by that time? Trip's hand could mend enough for him to keep doctoring out here. The firecracker fuse of passion between them could fizzle out as quickly as it had sizzled. Anything could happen. Anything.

And nothing. If Trip continued to see himself as helpless and useless, nothing further could happen between them. He'd sell his practice. She'd go on to the next relief job. After that, he'd . . . what would he do?

"I have to go in," he said into the uneasy silence that hung between them. "Nature calls."

Brenna nodded and handed him his crutch.

"I want to see how far I can get by myself," he said after she helped him to his feet.

Trip made it unaided all the way to the back door, a major feat. Aided by Brenna, he made it to the door of his bathroom. "I'll put the rest of the ice cream away," she told him at the door. "Try giving yourself a sponge bath. I'll come back in and wash wherever you can't reach."

She took his curt nod for the grudging agreement it was and herded the Dwarves out of the room with her.

Wounded soldier falls temporarily in love with his wartime nurse, Trip lectured himself as he ran warm water into the bathroom sink. *Nurse oversympathizes and falls temporarily in love with her besotted patient.*

Grade-B war movie or real life, the plot was hackneyed and predictable. Only on the silver screen did hero and heroine live happily ever after. Fade to credits.

"How's it going?" Brenna called through his room from the hall.

"Fine."

"Need me yet?"

"Not yet."

"I'll go change, then."

"No hurry." *Change into what?* Trip soaped, rinsed and dried his face, neck and torso. Bending to reach lower than his upper thigh, however, was impossible for him, as was washing his own back. Damned ribs. And forget about washing his one good arm with his one good hand. A true physical impossibility. Everywhere he could reach, including crucial private parts, he had reached.

Except for one. He took surgical scissors from the medicine chest and cut off his gauze head bandage. Worse than a punk rocker or clown, he decided, when his matted hair and the shaved gash on one side of his head were revealed. That wide swath was prickly now with new growth. In a couple of months he'd look normal from the neck up. Until then, he wouldn't be modeling for *Esquire*.

"You need a haircut," was Brenna's only reaction after her initial gasp when he called her in.

"I was fancying a safety pin in one ear, myself," Trip rejoined, noting that she'd changed from her swimsuit into a pink sleeveless shift that was as becoming as everything else she'd ever worn in his presence.

She returned his appraising glance in the mirror and advised, "Leave the hardware to the heavy-metal types. How does your head feel?"

"Free at last." He worked a comb through his hair. "And filthy."

"How clean are you otherwise?"

"So-so. All that's left is my back and leg."

Brenna raised her eyebrows. "Not bad. Once your ribs heal, you won't even need a nurse."

"Just do the honors, Nurse, and dispense with the pep talk."

Seeing a hint of a smile on his lips as he said it, Brenna gave him a mock salute. "Yes, sir, Dr. Hart. Right away."

She worked down from his shoulders to his waist and halted there. "Trip . . . ?"

"What?"

"You need dry—uh, clothes."

He cleared his throat. "I know. I got wetter every time I swished the washcloth around in there. But I'm cleaner there than anywhere," he claimed defensively, as if he half expected her to conduct an inspection and find him wanting.

"I believe it," she assured him. "Sit tight for a sec. I'll get a fresh pair."

"Top drawer on the—"

"I remember from before." She handed him his crutch. "Get balanced on this. I'll be back." But she stopped and turned at the door. "Would you rather wear something else?"

"Only if you can dig up something without zippers, buttons or snaps that'll stretch over Big Ben here," he said, rapping his knuckles against the top of his leg cast.

"Forget I asked."

"Wouldn't I love to. I hate this part," he said through gritted teeth, fitting his crutch to his armpit. "You would, too, I guarantee it."

Brenna didn't argue. After what had happened on the chaise, she had no basis for claiming again that skin was skin, as she had last night. There was nothing generic about even a single square inch of Trip. Stemming the steamy tide of that thought, she returned with a pair of cotton-knit briefs identical to the ones he wore.

"I'll stay behind you, okay?"

"Fine. Great."

She eased the first pair down his leg and his cast and slid them out from under him, one limb at a time. Reversing that sequence, she slipped the clean pair on. When they were up all the way, she snapped the wide elastic briefly against his lower back.

"There. Perfect."

Trip opened the eyes he'd kept shut tight during the entire maneuver. Only by thinking the most hideous thoughts had he quelled the reaction that threatened in his lower body. He had to keep thinking hideous even after Brenna had begun sweeping the soapy washcloth up and down his leg.

His leg was magnificent, Brenna thought. Straight, muscled, strong, incredibly masculine. His stride before the accident had been a long one. She reached around Trip to rinse the washcloth and felt a tiny tremor pass through him. A quick glance to the mirror showed her the sudden jut of his chin. She saw his eyes squeeze shut until the skin at the two outer corners crinkled.

"I'm almost done," she murmured, unsure whether she meant to reassure Trip or herself of an imminent end to the bittersweet torture of touch. With hasty hands she rinsed and dried him.

"How are my burns?" Trip mumbled.

Brenna set the towel aside and scanned his back. "They're . . ." She sucked in a breath. *Gone?*

"Uglier than a dog with a terminal case of mange?"

"They're . . ." Stunned, she touched the fingers of one hand to Trip's left shoulder where the reddest welt had been. Gone. She stared at her hand. No. This wasn't possible. She hadn't felt a thing when she'd smeared the cream on him earlier. No rush of heat. No tingling.

"I get the message. Here." Trip held the jar of cream over his shoulder. He could tell from her expression in the mirror that she might have jumped his bones once, but she wouldn't be doing it twice. Sure, the burns had been there when she jumped, but they had also been out of sight. Now her memory had been refreshed. Top it all off with a Halloween fright wig and what could a man expect?

Brenna snatched her hand away from him and took the cream. Gone. Healed. She couldn't say it, wouldn't say it. Like her ex-colleagues in San Jose, he'd say she could take her magic touch elsewhere, thank you. She swallowed hard and began to dab cream on at random.

"Do . . . does that hurt?"

"Nope. In fact, I'd forgotten I had them until I noticed the cream here where we left it this morning. It must be doing some good."

Brenna nodded, hoping that was the case. Always, in the past, she had felt *some* sensation in her hands, however slight it might have been. This morning she had felt nothing. Yet there were his back and shoulders, smooth and unmarred. Until now, such things had only happened with sick or injured animals. And then only when her concentration on treating the animal had been so intense that she had forgotten herself.

Even on such occasions, she reflected, the energy didn't always emerge from wherever it came. Nor did it always cure. More often her energized touch soothed, calmed, banished an animal's fear to a far greater extent than her normal touch did, given the same outer circumstances. *Open the door*, Howmedica had said in their last visit together before Brenna departed for the ranch. *Open the door.*

"Who's at the door?" Trip asked.

Brenna shook herself back to the present. "What?"

"The back door."

"Hey," Dwight's deep voice boomed. "Anybody home?" There was the sound of the screen door being bucked against the frame.

Brenna jammed the cap onto the jar in her hand. "I latched it to keep Byron and Malia out."

"Who invited *you* here, Bad-Boy?" Trip yelled out the bathroom window.

"*I* did, Hart-of-Stone."

"Leave a hinge or two on the door, will ya?"

"Who do you think you're locking out of this pile of boards you call a bachelor pad?"

"Pigs, man, pigs!"

"Same to you, Porky. Open up!"

Brenna wiped her hands on the towel and threw it aside. "Do you two always sweet-talk each other like this?"

"Only when we're getting along."

She rolled her eyes. "I'd hate to see you when you weren't. I'll get the door. Can you . . . ?" She gestured at the bed.

Trip frowned at her. "You saw me get out of it. I'll make it back the same way. Let him in before I have to buy a new door."

"I didn't say he could drop by when I saw him earlier. Are you sure you want company?"

"Only Dwight. He's like family. I'll tell him not to spread the word that I'm home yet. Otherwise, there'll be a steady stream through here and I'd rather—" He cut short his words, having almost said he'd rather be with *her* than anyone else he knew.

"Rather what?"

"Get a haircut before I face the crowd. I'll have to take enough bullsh—er—garbage about it from Dwight, as it is."

Dwight's first words when Brenna reached the door were, "Do I need a shrink or are two pigs in that pool?"

She flipped the latch and let him in, pleased to see that he was wearing a shirt. "Ask Trip. He'll tell you all about it."

"Where is he?"

"In bed."

"Lita around?"

"She's coming back later." Trip could tell him that story, too.

"For dinner?"

"No. She's made other plans for tonight."

"Entirely on purpose, if I know Lita. She does love striking a match." He nodded knowingly. "So it's just the vet and the relief vet all alone at the ranch."

"Shall I show you in, Dwight?"

"Nah. I know the way. I also know when I've been chilled out." He put on a mock hangdog expression and started across the kitchen.

"Dwight—"

He stopped and turned. "I'll keep it short. I promise."

"Thanks. And don't rag him about his hair."

"Me? Give my best friend a bad time?" He gave her a thumbs-up and disappeared down the hall.

The next thing she heard was a piercing wolf whistle and Dwight hooting, "*Hooeee.* Blind my eyes. Who's your new barber, Doc? Freddie the Slasher?"

7

TRIP WAS STILL ASLEEP. Brenna could see him from where she stood in his bedroom doorway. He had dozed off right after Dwight's red pickup crunched out of the driveway. It was now nearing sundown, and she was starving.

Holding her breath, she tiptoed in and looked down at him. Earlier she had done the same thing and gently drawn the sheet up over him as far as his waist. He didn't appear to have stirred since then except to fling the sheet off in the heat of the afternoon. He lay on his back, his hand splayed palm down on his stomach. Along with his hand, his entire forearm rose and fell with his breathing.

Brenna gazed at his face. He looked so relaxed and untroubled in the sweet escape sleep provided from pain and worry. Above the strong planes of his cheekbones, his thick lashes were dark crescents. His lips were slightly open to the ebb and flow of his breath. The five-o'clock shadow of his beard stood in harsh contrast to his hospital-pale skin.

Had he been a twice-a-day shaver before even once a day became a left-handed trial? As she wondered, it came to her that the perfect gift for him might be an electric shaver. If Lita didn't beat her to it.

Lita. Brenna had sneaked out to Trip's office and called her after he fell asleep. No answer. A second call an hour later was no more successful. Brenna's great worry was that Trip would be left alone if an emergency call came in and she had to leave. Without Lita to depend on, who was there? Dwight was the nearest neighbor, but it was highly unlikely he'd be home to take a call on Fourth of July eve.

She supposed she could try Trip's sister, Elena, who lived fifty miles away with her husband and children. But two preschoolers wouldn't be easy to leave, even for an emergency. Trip's other sister, Bianca, lived in Santa Fe, New Mexico, so she wasn't even a possibility.

Brenna told herself not to worry. The office line hadn't rung all weekend. Holidays, even in more populated areas than this, were traditionally slow. Animals fell sick and got injured, though, holiday or not. She, and every vet she knew, could tell heartrending tales of the Thanksgivings, Christmases and New Years they had missed because the phone rang or the pager beeped in the middle of everything.

Only relieving the pain and repairing the damage made the sacrifices worthwhile. Losing the battle with death on a holiday was the real heartbreaker. That hurt a caring vet, in most cases, much more than missing turkey and pumpkin pie, the opening of gifts, the midnight toast and Auld Lang—

"Run!"

Trip's sudden, strangled shout jolted Brenna's heart into her throat.

"Run, damn you!" His fist punched out, hitting her square in the thigh. "Outta here! Now! Outta—"

Brenna grabbed his wrist before he could land a second blow. "Trip! Wake up!"

His upper body jackknifed up from the mattress. "Beat it. Go!"

"It's me, Trip. Brenna."

Trip's eyes flashed open, unseeing, filled with fear. Then realizing where he was, he fell back to his pillow. "Aarrgh," he gasped, crushing Brenna's hand in his. "My ribs..." He groaned, overcome with pain.

"Shh. Stay still." Brenna sat down on the bed and smoothed a trembling hand over his damp forehead. "Shh. It was only a dream. I'm here."

"Brenna—"

"Hush. Catch your breath." She eased her aching hand from his and propped his shoulders up with more pillows. "Is that better?"

He nodded, his throat working, his eyes blinking, his breath shallow and broken. "Brenna...I..." He covered his eyes with his hand and swallowed hard. "I...the deer... it wouldn't run. I yelled...and pushed...but it wouldn't—"

"It's safe, Trip. You saved it."

He pressed his thumb and forefinger against his eyelids. "I dream it over and over." His chest heaved and he breathed forth a racking sigh.

Brenna's eyes brimmed with tears. Gently she lifted his hand from his furrowed brow and twined her fingers with his. "You're safe, too," she murmured over and over until he quieted. She brushed a tear from the corner of his eye and one from her own. "Home safe."

"Home, yes." He sighed thankfully and then opened his eyes. "What time is it?"

"Time for dinner."

"Dinner. I've been dead to the world all this time?"

Brenna nodded and squeezed his hand. "Hungry?"

"I don't know. I guess so." He thought for two seconds and squeezed back. "Yeah. Starved."

"Good. There's a steak in the kitchen with your name on it."

Trip's face fell. "You already ate?"

"No. There's one with *my* name on it, too. Would you like a glass of wine while they're cooking?"

"Yeah. I could use something to bring me back."

"Can I get you anything else? A book to read? TV? Byron and Malia?"

He brightened at those two names. "Where are they?"

"Having a frozen juice bar party on the patio."

"I'd invite myself to it, but I'm not up to making the trip right now."

"In that case, I'll invite the party to *you*." She stood up and reluctantly released Trip's hand. Just as reluctantly, it seemed, his fingers parted from hers.

"Don't tear them away from a good time just for me."

Brenna laughed. "Between you and a juice bar, there's no contest. Brace yourself for the thundering herd."

Thunder Malia and Byron did—straight down the hall and onto the bed where they snuffled soft greetings into Trip's hand and flopped over on their backs for a massage.

"If you ever get tired of them, I'm the first bidder," Trip said when Brenna brought him his wine.

"I might give it a thought the next time Halley's comet sails around. In the meantime, I'll go ruin the steaks. For what it's worth, how do you like yours?"

"Let's see . . ." He stopped stroking Malia's tummy to rub his chin and purse his lips. "Ruined sounds edible, but medium will do, too."

"I'll make it up to you with peach cobbler," Brenna promised with an apologetic smile before she left him.

Trip watched her go. Hell, he'd eat charcoal if Brenna Deveney was serving it up. She was one first-rate woman, forthright and frank, fun to be with, feminine, caring—and sexy. No, sexy wasn't word enough for what she was in that sense. Brenna was more, in every sense, than mere words could describe.

He sipped his wine, swirling it on his tongue. It wasn't the vintage's deep red richness or spicy character that he savored, however. It was the remembered taste of Brenna's mouth, more intoxicating than any wine he'd ever tasted. He craved more.

"You lucky devils," he muttered to Byron and Malia. "I'll bet you sleep with her every night."

Malia sighed and Byron echoed her, as if confirming that Trip was entirely correct and could eat his heart out.

Trip sighed, too, and polished off his wine. Kissing Brenna was one thing. Sleeping with her in the fullest sense of that word would be entirely another. *I've been thinking about it for two weeks*, he remembered her saying of their kiss. Well. She must have also been thinking that kissing was about as far as things could go. She wasn't blind. Neither was he. Any man with a mouth could kiss. It took a man with his physical powers in prime form to fully make love with a woman.

Not that all of his physique at peak performance level had kept Suzanne at home. Her shrewd, money-grubbing guru had lured her away. Compared to that flashy new age con man, plain old Trip Hart had not measured up.

"I hope steak and tossed salad is enough," Brenna said, coming in with a tray a while later. "We're out of potatoes and French bread."

"The apology is mine. You weren't expecting company."

"No, but I'm glad to have it." She made the pigs get down before she set Trip's tray next to him on the bed and went back to the kitchen to get hers. Knowing better than to beg, Byron and Malia wriggled under the bed and went back to sleep.

Trip looked at his plate and closed his eyes. Brenna had been wrong about ruining his steak, he thought. It was perfect. Each bite-sized piece she had cut for him was plump, pink and oozing with juice.

"I knew it." Brenna made a self-deprecating face and set down the TV tray that held her dinner and the bottle of Petite Sirah. "It's bleeding too much, isn't it?"

Without opening his eyes, he shook his head.

"Not bleeding enough, then. That's what you get when the cook likes hers burned to a crisp. I warned you. I'm no good unless I'm cooking my own. Fletcher liked his still mooing. I never could get it right."

Trip forced his eyes open. "You got it perfect this time."

"You're kidding."

"It's perfect."

Brenna pulled a chair to her TV tray and sat down. "If it's perfect, what's wrong?"

"Nothing. Refill?" He held out his wineglass.

She filled his and her own and picked up her knife and fork. "That dream's still bothering you, isn't it?"

Trip nodded. It was, a little. What loomed larger and twice as daunting, though, was this glimpse he was now getting of a future of precut steaks, chops and roasts. If he couldn't wield a knife and fork at dinner, wielding a scalpel and probe in surgery was out of the question.

Seeing his yearning look at the utensils she held, Brenna caught the drift of his thoughts. She set her knife and fork down. "You aren't the only one I've carved a steak for in the past two weeks," she said. "Your mother had the same problem with her sprain at first."

"She won't be that way for the rest of her life."

"You won't be in that cast for the rest of yours, either. When does it come off?"

He shrugged and picked up his fork. "Jamison says three weeks, give or take. Longer for the leg. I have no feeling, though." He took a bite of steak. "Can't move my fingers or toes."

"You can move the arm, though."

He nodded. "Out and up from the shoulder joint. Back and forth a little." He took another bite and seemed anxious to change the subject. "This is good."

"And you can move your leg at the hip," Brenna prodded, undeterred from accentuating the positive.

"I'm dead meat from the knee down." He forked up some salad. "Great dressing."

"Will you need a leg brace once you're out of the cast?"

"Not as badly as I'll need a job." He gave her a resolute look. "What kind of dressing is it?"

Brenna gave up. "Ranch style. Made with yogurt."

"Yuck." He stared at his salad bowl. "I hate yogurt."

"You didn't a minute ago. What's wrong with it?"

"Nothing, it just reminds me of . . ."

She took a bite of salad and waited.

"Among a million other fads, Suzanne got into health food before we split," he finally explained, resuming his meal. "Vegetarian, organic, macrobiotic, yin, yang, bee pollen, nothing cooked, everything raw, no protein on Tuesday, carbohydrates only during a new moon. It made crazy sense, in a way, since she couldn't cook. I couldn't stomach it, though. Plain yogurt and seaweed on mung-bean toast wasn't my idea of dinner."

"According to Lita you're the enchiladas and tamales and burritos type."

"Lead me to them," said Trip, smiling. His smile faded. "Mexican soul food, even meatless, wasn't vegetarian enough for Suzanne. Nothing here was enough for her after she fell in with that crackpot bunch."

"Lita says they're not that bad. Just spacey and ... different."

"'On a different path, marching to a different drum,'" Trip quoted his mother. "I can hear her now. It was Suzanne who got her into yoga, you know."

"I know. She loves it."

"Why am I even bothering? You've heard it all before from Mom, haven't you?"

"Not all of it. Just the bare bones of what happened and that Suzanne had always been ..."

"Flighty?"

"Something like that." Lita's precise words had been "a real space cadet."

"She was a butterfly, all right, flitting from life-style to life-style as if the world were a perennial flower garden. I was twenty-nine when she flitted into mine. Old enough to know better, but convinced I was the flower she'd been searching for."

"How did you meet?"

"Mom didn't ...?"

"She only said Suzanne wasn't from around here."

"Far from it." Trip nudged a lettuce leaf around his bowl with his fork. "Boulder, Colorado. She had moved there from the Bahamas by way of Manhattan. She was in her Rocky-Mountain-High phase at the time. I'd gone to a national vet conference in Denver. Dropped into Boulder to visit a friend. His girlfriend and Suzanne were roommates. Instant foursome for dinner."

Instant attraction, too, Brenna was thinking. Trip's photo album had shown both his ex-wife and daughter to be wispy, fairylike beauties with huge blue eyes and floating clouds of wavy dark hair that trailed away into the air behind them. It hadn't been difficult for Brenna to imagine Suzanne sprouting iridescent wings and fluttering blithely away in search of a sweeter nectar.

"As restless as a hummingbird," Lita had told Brenna as they pored over the album together. "I knew right away they were wrong for each other. Her parents were dead. She was alone in the world. She filled his need to rescue a homeless thing and shelter it. He filled her need to be grounded in reality until her next flight. They had nothing to build a marriage on. It went downhill from the start."

"When I told her about the house and the ranch," Trip continued, "she got all starry-eyed. Raved about how she adored ranches and cattle. Craved a garden so she could can vegetables and make jam. Wanted to get back to the earth. I got starry-eyed, too, listening to her. She flew back with me and we were married two months later. Aura was born that year. The year after that, Suzanne sued for primary custody of Aura, and won."

"I'm glad Fletch and I didn't have custody to fight over," Brenna commented. "It was bad enough knowing what he'd gone through with his second wife on the issue."

Trip stared into his wineglass, then took a drink. "I lost the fight because I'm a vet. Unlike Suzanne, I get called away at all hours for emergencies. Not a stable presence in my child's daily life, the court decided." He snorted in disbelief. "The only thing the judge and I agreed on is that Aura must attend public school. That much of her life, at least, is mainstream American. The rest of it . . ." He shook his head as if clearing it of a bad memory. "Don't let me get started on that damned commune. There are nicer ways to ruin a good dinner."

Brenna smiled sympathetically. "Lita mentioned that it was best not to bring up the subject when you're in a bad mood."

"Even in a good mood," Trip growled, "I've never had anything kind to say about that new-age kook the mother of my child calls her soul-mate savior. And I never will. Without him and his crankcase ideas, she might have stuck around here after divorcing me."

Brenna frowned. "I thought she divorced you *because* of him."

"She did," Trip bitterly acknowledged. "She even married that spiritual fraud. *I'd* have preferred a rival I could respect. If she had betrayed me with someone who lived around here, I could see Aura now on a regular basis."

And Suzanne, too? she wondered. Was he still in love with her? Brenna knew firsthand how it felt to be long on loyalty, yet sold short on love by a spouse. The coed Fletcher had dumped her for had been a vain sorority vamp who had used him to raise her grade-point average. Brenna still smarted when comparing herself to that flippant little wench, just as Trip obviously still smarted when comparing himself to Suzanne's self-styled savior. Brenna, however, knew she didn't love Fletcher anymore. She loved Trip. And the emotion was taking deeper root, minute by minute. If Trip still loved Suzanne . . .

"You love her?" she murmured before she could stop herself.

"Of course. I love Aura more than my life. But not Suzanne." He heard the sharper emphasis he put on the latter statement. It was important for Brenna to know that. He didn't want her thinking that he still . . . still what? He brought the dangling thought up short and reeled it in. What difference did it make what she knew about who he did or didn't love? It wasn't as if anyone's future was at stake here, he reminded himself. As a man with a dim outlook ahead, he had to remember that. Love and romance were luxuries he couldn't afford anymore.

He concentrated on finishing his steak, painfully aware at the same time of his immense romantic attraction to the woman who had cooked it to such juicy perfection. Brenna was everything Suzanne had not been. Not only did she know her way around a kitchen, as well as a surgery, but she was a strong individual who took her responsibilities seriously.

Here sat a woman a man could depend on when he needed to, instead of carrying the whole load himself. A woman, not a girl. Not an impossible dreamer like Suzanne who had burned the bottoms out of ten tea kettles in three years because she "forgot . . . just forgot . . . y'know?" Trip could still visualize her saying that in her breathy voice with her ditzy smile and a daydreamy wave of her pale, blue-veined hand. What had he ever seen in her?

"I'd better check on the cobbler," Brenna said, and rose. "Are you finished?"

Trip cocked an eyebrow at her. "Do you see even a crumb on my plate?"

"Just thought I'd ask before grabbing." She flushed, thinking that grabbing more than just his plate would be nice. A quick kiss would be a much sweeter dessert than even the cobbler promised to be.

"They grab at the hospital, whether you're finished or not," Trip said. "Most of the time I never started, so it was no big loss." He eyed his empty plate in her hand and winked at her. "I'm going to get fat if you keep this up."

"Get used to it. I like to cook."

"A woman after my own heart."

She stacked her plate on his and winked back. "Keep up the sweet talk and you'll get more than just dessert."

In former days, in former times, he might have run a fingertip down her arm and seductively suggested, "Let's skip dessert, then." Her answer to that might have been a dulcet laugh that agreed they'd best do that with the greatest of haste.

"Dwight's the sweet-talker. Not me," he replied, settling back with a shrug at what he might have done but could no longer do, given the circumstances. Why court the ultimate rejection with sweet talk? *A woman after my own heart.* He should never have said it.

Brenna shrugged, too, to hide her chagrin that Trip had backtracked without warning out of the flirty exchange he'd initiated. Damn him. She didn't appreciate being lured out like that and left batting her eyelashes at thin air.

In the kitchen, she rinsed the dishes and silverware with a clatter, muttering to herself. If he wanted to be that way, let him. She wouldn't snap like a hungry trout at his bait a second time. If he wanted her, he could go for it like any other red-blooded male who wanted a woman badly enough to make a move he couldn't retract.

She had made enough moves herself, thank you. And enough excuses for Trip Hart. So his wife had left him for another man. He had a lot of company in the world on that score. So he was laid up in bed. That particular lemon could be transformed into lemonade. After all, what better place than the bed he was in for a seduction scenario?

She pulled the crusty, fragrant cobbler out of the oven. He could eat his share of it alone, she decided. She had put too much on hold for him already. She had enough paperwork to fill several hours and enough unread veterinary research journals to keep her reading past midnight.

She only wished she'd had enough kissing for one day.

"Would you like coffee with this?" she asked when she took Trip his plate of cobbler.

He glanced from his plate to her. "Don't you get some of this, too?"

"I'm going for a walk."

"Oh."

Hearing their favorite four-letter word, the two pigs scooted out from under the bed, ready for an evening stroll.

"Coffee?" Brenna repeated. *Tea? Me?*

"No, thanks."

She followed the pigs to the door. "I won't be gone long, if the phone rings."

"Sure." A walk. What he wouldn't give. A winding country road. Chirping crickets in the fields. The full moon like a gigantic pearl in the night sky. If only he had two legs to walk in the moonlight with her! "Have a good one."

"You'll be okay till I get back?"

He sank his fork into his cobbler. "What could happen to me in bed?"

More than you seem to want to think. "Well, see ya later."

Trip was fast asleep when Brenna returned much later. She drew the sheet over him and tiptoed out with his empty dessert plate.

Her lengthy walk hadn't helped. She was still restless enough to putter in the kitchen, wish the phone would ring with an emergency, hope it *wouldn't* ring. Deserting the kitchen for the parlor, she settled onto the horse-hair sofa with Byron and Malia and leafed partway through a research journal before setting it aside to stare into space.

Malia nuzzled her little head into Brenna's right thigh and peered up at her with dark, quizzical eyes. Byron nuzzled up to her left thigh and gazed at her with the same expression.

"You're sleeping with me, as usual," she replied in answer to the burning question in their eyes. "Thanks for being good kids last night and sleeping in the infirmary. And no, you cannot sleep on Trip's bed tonight, no matter how hard you beg."

Malia wrinkled her nose and Byron snuffled a soft grunt of protest.

"Even the Dwarves can't sleep there tonight. Trip needs all the rest he can get. Later on, when he's feeling better, okay?"

Another wrinkle. Another grunt.

Brenna heaved a long, frustrated sigh. "I know. I want to sleep with him, too."

MONDAY MORNING WAS HOTTER than the day before. After a cool shower, Brenna dressed in blue tropical-print shorts and a matching halter top and checked on Trip.

"Off to Waikiki without me?" he inquired when she walked in.

"I'll send postcards," she promised. "What would you like to do today?"

"Lie on the coral sands with you, sipping piña coladas and watching the surf roll in."

"How about a shampoo and haircut, instead?"

"Are you the barber?"

Brenna propped her hands on her hips and pursed her lips. "No. Byron volunteered and Malia offered to assist."

"I'm theirs, then. All I'd have gotten on the beach is sunburned. Might as well get shampooed and sheared instead."

"Outside after breakfast. You can practice shaving yourself again, too."

"I'll be there. It's like hell in here. I could use a few slaves with fans."

"Air conditioning would be kinder. Why don't you have it?"

"It's only like this four or five days out of every summer. No one was predicting a drought this year."

"I see. Do you feel like sunny-side up today or scrambled?"

"Scrambled."

"With salsa, toast and coffee?"

"Might as well, since I'm paying you double for the weekend."

"Paying me what?"

"Twice the going rate. For taking care of me."

"Trip—"

He held up his hand. "Save your breath. I write the paychecks here."

She was forced to save it. The phone rang. Trip picked it up.

"*Buenos días* to you, too," he replied after answering. "Still mad at the only son you'll ever have in your whole, entire life?"

Brenna went to scramble eggs. Thank heaven Lita had surfaced. Would she be coming out today? There was no telling. In a way, she hoped Lita would stay put. As frustrating as it was, Brenna liked caring for Trip and being with him—and him alone. She hadn't lived with any man day and night since Fletch. She hadn't wanted to until now.

"TAKE THE REST OF THE DAY off, *amiga*," Lita urged when she arrived right after Trip finished breakfast. "Drive over to Pismo Beach where it's cool and build sand castles with the *poquitos*. You need some time to yourself and I need time with Trip."

Unable to argue with a mother's prerogative, Brenna took herself and her pigs off on the long drive to San Luis Obispo. It was certainly cooler, she had to admit, when she reached the turnoff to Pismo Beach. It was cooler still at the beach. Freezing, actually, was more accurate. Pea-soup fog shrouded the entire scene. Byron and Malia took one look out the car window, and refused to get out.

Brenna groaned, and drove back to San Luis where the sun still shone, though less brightly as high fog began to roll in from the sodden coast. What to do, though, with two pigs in a sleepy university town on July the Fourth?

The three ended up having their picnic in a bucolic cow pasture on the way back to the ranch.

"I don't know about you," Brenna said to Byron and Malia in the pasture, "but I'd rather be shaving Trip."

His name was all they had to hear to perk right up and head for the car.

The afternoon shadows were long when Brenna turned into the gravel driveway. Under the oak tree Lita sat in the lawn chair and Trip in the chaise. From all appearances, Lita's wrist was back in working order again.

"Where's your tan?" was Trip's greeting.

"Where's your hair?" was Brenna's reply. It hurt a little to see that he'd been shaved, shampooed, sheared and blown dry by loving hands other than her own. That dimple, that cleft chin, razored by someone else.

"You like?" inquired Lita, glancing from her handiwork to Brenna. "Or don't like?"

"Nice job," Brenna approved with a smile as mild as she could manage. Barbered or unbarbered, Trip was one outstanding piece of work. She liked, all right. But she wasn't going to stand there in front of him and his mother looking as hot and bothered about him as she felt.

"Well, I'm off," Lita announced, rising from her seat.

"You're not staying for dinner?" Brenna asked, suppressing a smile of pure delight.

"No. But I brought it, *amiga*. The cheese enchiladas are in the oven. And tomorrow we go back to work, *sí*?"

"Were there any calls while I was gone?"

Trip shook his head. "All clear, so far."

"Good night, *muchacha*." Lita kissed Trip, hugged Brenna, got into her car and drove away.

Trip glanced at Brenna, who stood watching Lita disappear. "Do you *really* like?"

Brenna glanced down. "Very much. You look like a cover for *Gentleman's Quarterly*."

"*Hospital Quarterly*'s more like it," he demurred, smiling a little despite himself. "How was the beach?"

"Dripping with fog." She sighed and sat down in the lawn chair. "I wish I hadn't gone."

"You'd rather continue the rip-roaring good time you've been having here all weekend, I take it."

She turned to him. "Fog or no fog, I'd rather have been here in the kiddie pool with my pigs—and you. What's so hard to believe about that?"

"I . . . I'd rather be here, too. I just . . ."

"Don't worry," Brenna said, standing again. "I won't get so attached to you and this place that I won't know when to leave."

"What worries me," Trip said haltingly to her back, "is that you'll leave before . . ."

She turned around warily. "Before what, Trip?"

"I'm—not sure." He bowed his head and lowered his gaze to his leg cast. "I missed you like crazy today. That's all I know."

8

I MISSED YOU, TOO, TRIP. Brenna wanted to say it. Remembering how swiftly Trip could snap his neck in after sticking it out, however, she bit back the words.

But she did sit down in the lawn chair again in wary acknowledgment of what he'd said.

A hot breeze ruffled the tree leaves and the edge of the quilt on Trip's chaise. His dark red hair, shorter and neater now, stirred in the buoyant air. Brenna tucked the sides of her own hair behind her ears and lifted her face to the breeze. In a bush nearby, a flock of sparrows bickered. Overhead, a lone hawk soared in a grand sweep above the sundown-shadowed hills of the ranch.

Trip cleared his throat. "We polished off the rest of the peach ice cream for lunch."

Brenna waited in vain for him to make a second step forward after that step back. Finally she said, "You and Lita got your differences settled?"

"In all of two minutes. I take after her side of the family when I lose it. We both go off like fireworks when we irk each other, but the smoke clears fast." He chuckled. "It took longer this time because I called her a matchmaker the other day. I almost had to get on my knees to apologize. Only the cast saved me."

"Everything's back to normal, then?"

"Not quite. Two things still need to be straightened out."

"There's no use worrying about your arm and leg until the casts come off," Brenna said with a philosophic shrug.

He was silent for a moment. "I didn't mean that. I meant us."

Brenna watched Malia leap with a splash into the wading pool. Byron followed with a splash. She kept her eyes on them. "What about us?"

"Good question."

"You brought it up."

"We both did. Yesterday."

Brenna turned to look at him. "I told you I have no regrets about what happened yesterday."

"I do."

Trip looked serious and almost angry. She looked away. "Why?"

"I'm falling in love with you."

It seemed a small eternity before Brenna could draw breath again. Another condensed eon passed before her heartbeat took up where it had stopped. Her mind, immobilized in midthought, resumed movement only after her blood began to course again. What Trip had uttered, she realized, were words too serious to be snatched back.

"I know," he said ruefully, studying her stunned profile. "I've been home a grand total of two days and I'm already way ahead of you. It's a classic symptom of my unfortunate condition, if those war movies about cripples and nurses can be believed."

Brenna twisted in her chair to face him. "Has it occurred to you that I'm the one who's been running in place, hoping *you'd* catch up?"

"Briefly. That's a symptom, too, I suspect."

"Of what?"

"Of the sympathetic side of your nature. Your capacity to mistake empathy for something it isn't has already been documented."

"You're the one making the mistake," Brenna returned, rising from her chair and towering over him. "That was no trite Tinseltown script we acted out yesterday. It was basic big-time sexual attraction. And I can only speak for myself when I say sex minus love isn't my style."

"It's not mine, either," he conceded, "but what I've been feeling for you isn't what half a man should realistically be feeling for a whole woman like you."

She raised an eyebrow in patent frustration. "That wasn't half a kiss we indulged in yesterday."

"Love doesn't stop at kissing. And frankly, neither does sex, while we're on the subject."

"Let's *both* be frank, then, Trip. You aren't a eunuch. Far from it—as we both know."

"I'm not what I used to be." He shot her a dark glance. "Far from it—as we both know."

Brenna heaved a loud sigh and sank down onto her knees next to the chaise. "Trip Hart, listen to me." She took his hand and clasped it between hers. "You have my unqualified permission to feel whatever you feel for me, and—"

"I can't—"

She touched a silencing finger to his lips. "And in return I want your permission to feel what I feel for you. To be entirely honest and aboveboard, I think you're the sexiest, most desirable man I've ever known. I want to make love *with* you and *to* you." So this was how it felt to throw caution to the wind, she thought with a thrill. It was like spreading wings and taking flight.

She drew his arm around her waist and held it there, the position pushing her breasts up and out against her halter. "I have no illusions about what you can and can't do in your condition. I know we'd have to be very creative until you're out of those casts."

Flying high now, she leaned into him and pressed her lips to his for a fleeting second. "Very creative. Day in and day out, I think about the things we could do. How we could do them. When and where."

"Brenna," Trip said in a hoarse whisper, "if you're trifling with me . . ."

She murmured, "I'm not trifling. When the casts come off, we'll explore our options again...and exercise every one we can."

Trip's hand, already gripped to hers behind her back, pulled her against him. He breathed in her soap-clean scent and gazed into her amber eyes. "I hope you know what you're getting into," he breathed. "One of us should."

She slid her fingers through his freshly cut hair and wrapped them around the back of his neck. "I know what I'm doing and I know what I want. Kiss me again, Trip...."

Their mouths melted together, hot and needy, giving, taking, softly sucking, spiraling the heat between them into a fire storm of desire.

In one fluid motion, without breaking the exquisite suction, Brenna slid onto her side on the chaise next to Trip. She angled her uppermost leg over his cast and gave him everything he wanted of her mouth while taking everything she wanted of his. She felt his hand roam her bare back, felt his fingers loop under the back tie of her halter top. With an arch of her spine, she wordlessly invited him to tug it loose.

He moaned and pulled. Another strong tug released the tie around her neck. The brief tropical-print garment fell away, leaving her breasts bare against Trip's equally bare chest.

He tore his mouth from hers, gasping, "Brenna...I want you, but I can't..."

"You *can*," she encouraged against his lips. She levered up on one elbow to free his arm of her weight and skimmed the palm of her other hand over the hair on his chest. "You can reach out—" she stroked her fingertip over the sharp point of his nipple "—and touch..."

Trip shuddered, opened his eyes and looked at her. *"Linda sin comparación,"* he whispered, lapsing into Spanish at the sight of Brenna's full, rose-tipped breasts. Freckles formed tiny pinpoint dots on her creamy skin there.

"I hope that means you like freckles," Brenna murmured, sucking in a breath at the graze of Trip's knuckles down the slope of her right breast.

His hot dark gaze followed the movement of his hand. "It means 'beautiful without compare.' I more than like what I see." He cradled her in his palm and rotated his thumb around the rosy areola that drew into a tight pout at his touch.

Brenna trembled, moved by the rapt expression on his face, the flare of his nostrils as his fingers took their full measure and fill of her.

"Yes," she murmured, "yes...yes..." and lifted herself higher in the chaise until she felt the wondrous heat of his mouth pressed to her breast.

Trip heard Brenna's breath quiver and back up in her throat at the first flick of his tongue against her. He felt her shiver of response to the stimulus, the fine sheen of perspiration on her silky skin. She tasted fresh, feminine—and aroused. As wonderfully, wildly aroused as he was. He sucked her in, teased her swollen nipple with the tip of his tongue, let her go, blew softly where he had wet her.

"Brenna," he whispered, and drew her in again slow and deep, in and out. His fingers, now cupped to her other breast, plucked and stroked and squeezed.

Brenna had never received such pleasure from a man. Even in the heady dawn of their courtship, her English professor ex-husband had spouted erotic love poems with far more impassioned intensity than he had brought to bear in bed with her, either then or later. Poetry, not passion, had put starry-eyed Brenna in his thrall.

Now she discovered that a man's mouth could shape the most erotic of love poems without uttering a word. From Trip's teeth and tongue and lips alone she received the message that his personal style as a lover was intense, impassioned and uninhibited.

Trip felt delirious with the abundance of her breasts, her taste, the fevered play of her fingers in his hair, her sighs and soft moans that told him she couldn't get enough of what he was doing any more than he could get his fill of doing it. She was dynamite.

Even as he thought it, a blast split the air. They pulled apart and stared at each other. Byron and Malia leaped out of the pool and huddled under the chaise. A second blast followed, then the distant sound of raucous laughter and the squeal of tires as a car sped off down the road.

"What—?" Brenna's first disoriented thought was that she was topless in broad daylight. She bolted up from the chaise. Then she remembered the house was set too far back from the road for anyone to see her. She grabbed up her halter anyway.

"Reckless kids throwing cherry bombs," Trip said with a grimace.

"Scared me to death." Brenna clutched the halter protectively against her. "How do you know those were cherry bombs?"

"I was a reckless kid myself once on July the Fourth."

"Do cherry bombs set off fires?"

He nodded. "You'd better get out there and check, just in case."

"Fire. Just what we need," she muttered, tying the halter around her midriff and then fumbling with the neck tie.

"Mmm-hmm," Trip agreed. "The one we just started was almost too hot to handle."

"Don't let it burn out," she murmured with a sidelong glance at him that skimmed over his white briefs. "I'll be back."

"I'll be here. Doing a slow burn."

She ascertained that there was no fire where the smoke and litter of the cherry bombs still lingered and then raced back through the house only to hear the kitchen phone ringing. She frowned at it. *Ring. Ring.* It wouldn't stop.

Trip heard the ringing cease and Brenna exclaim, "Oh, no! Poor Trixie." He closed his eyes and willed himself to relax. So much for dynamite on the Fourth.

He was almost down to normal when the back door slammed and he heard her soft footfall on the grass.

"Trip?"

"Let me guess. Emergency?" He kept his eyes closed, knowing he'd rise up hot as a blowtorch if he so much as looked at her.

"It's the Pemberton's mare, Trixie. She has—"

"Colic," he cut in, his tone knowing and certain. "Ash and Cissy P. have houseguests, I imagine."

"He did mention that they have friends here from Manhattan. What does that have to do with Trixie?"

"Everything." He sighed and opened his eyes. "The Pembertons are San Francisco socialites. Always wanted a ranch. Bought Quail Hill last year. Their city friends come out and try to get Trixie to feed from their hands. They're more skittish around horses than most horses are around people and end up spilling half the feed because they're afraid she'll bite."

Brenna gave a nod of understanding. "I get the picture. Trixie scavenges the feed from the ground and swallows dirt and gravel. After too much scavenging, the indigestible grit collects in her stomach causing severe pain. If horses could upchuck, she'd take care of her own problem. They can't, though, so we do what we can. Diagnosis—impaction colic."

"Right on, Doctor," Trip said with a smile of approval. "She had the same problem last Christmas when the London friends were out. The Labor Day weekend before that it was the same story with the Palm Beach billionaires.

"Should I do a rectal first? Or use a stomach tube?"

Trip shook his head. "I've never had to do either. Trixie's high-strung. Once you get an analgesic into her, she calms down. The big problem's getting the syringe within ten feet of her."

Brenna swallowed hard. "I haven't treated equine colic since vet school. Refresh my memory."

"If you hear good loud gut sounds when you do your preliminary, try the shot first. Once she's calm, walk her around for a while. If that helps, keep walking her for the next few hours to move the obstruction along."

"Can I depend on Ash to help walk her?"

"Nope. All Ash does is pay the bill."

Brenna raised an eyebrow. "Does he pay it with good grace?"

"You bet. Hell of a way to spend a fortune, if you ask me, but easy come easy go when you have thirty million, I guess. I'm blue in the face from telling him not to let Trixie feed from the ground, and all it gets me is a fat fee."

"Can't the Pembertons control their friends?"

"Not after the house party starts with a champagne toast. It's nonstop bubbly up on the hill until the last guest leaves."

"In other words, duck the flying champagne glasses."

Trip grinned. "And the caviar spoons."

"Brother. I'd better help you in and get going."

"Quail Hill's a good hour's drive to and from on hairpin curves," Trip said, reaching for his crutch. "You won't be back until after midnight."

"Poor Trixie." Brenna helped him to his foot. "I'll call Lita to come back out."

"Poor Mom, too. Tending a sick kid again after all these years."

"That's what mothers are for."

"She'll stay overnight, you know," he said when they reached his bed.

"I know."

There was nothing then for either of them to say or do. Whatever might have been possible before the phone rang would be a certain impossibility with Trip's mother sleeping under the same roof.

CALMING TRIXIE WAS IMPOSSIBLE until after Ashley Pemberton exited the picture. The dainty gray mare was rolling on the floor of her dimly lit stall while a splashy fireworks display lit up the lawn. But fortunately, aristocratic Ashley, two sheets to the wind and stylish in designer whites, returned to his guests immediately after showing her to the stable and answering her questions about Trixie's condition.

Trixie, he told Brenna, had been rolling off and on for a couple of hours. He had tried to walk her around the paddock to ease her distress, but she had balked.

Brenna had the impression that he considered Trixie to be no different from a trendy automobile he might turn over to a mechanic for repair. If animals could talk, she thought, the tearful tales they'd tell. It was no wonder the little Arabian had balked at being led around by the man. Ashley should have stuck to fancy cars.

With him gone, the mare came unsteadily to her feet and allowed Brenna to approach with a stethoscope.

"There, girl. Easy now," Brenna crooned, stroking the velvet nose. "I'm just going to listen to your heart and take your pulse. Yes, I know you hurt inside."

Fast pulse, Brenna noted. Elevated heartbeat. She moved the stethoscope and heard loud gut sounds, the positive sign Trip had mentioned. Checking the inner lips and gums for shock, Brenna found them to be pink with only a tinge of red, another good sign.

With a guttural groan, Trixie sat back on her hind legs in an equine effort to ease her gastric distress. Brenna smoothed a hand down the slope of the mare's sweaty back—and then it happened. The energized heat. The subtle vibration.

Trixie craned her neck around and looked at Brenna, then sighed and sat motionless as the energy passed between them. *Feel, don't think* had been Howmedica's final instruction to her before she left San Jose. Brenna closed her eyes, let her mind go blank and went with the feeling.

She felt Trixie rise slowly to all fours again and go perfectly still once more.

Then, as suddenly as it had begun, the energy ceased. Trixie nickered and craned her neck to nuzzle Brenna's shoulder. Brenna opened her eyes and could have sworn the mare was smiling at her. She checked the pulse again and found it normal, as was the heartbeat. Only the encouraging gut sounds remained.

"Well," said Brenna, "you're not going to need that nasty old syringe now, are you?"

Trixie nickered again and stamped her forefoot twice.

Brenna smiled and led her out of the stall by the halter. "I'd like a walk, too, Trixie. A couple hundred rounds of the paddock should keep you off the floor—and pay a couple of Trip's hospital bills."

LITA MADE *HUEVOS RANCHEROS* for breakfast the next morning. Though normally the coffee-until-lunch type, Brenna ate a full plate of the spicy egg-tortilla dish to fortify herself. Even after three cups of strong coffee, she doubted she'd get through the full day of office appointments and house calls ahead with her eyes more than half-open.

Trip was still asleep when she and Lita opened his office for the first patients, a springer spaniel with a tick-infested ear and a tabby cat suffering from severe summer eczema. Next came a colorful Amazon parrot for a wing trim. Its owner had learned the hard way that a wing trim, when properly performed, kept a pet bird from injuring itself both in the house and out. The owner's first Amazon had flown through an open window and died from electrocution after landing on a power line.

Brenna did both reception and doctoring for the while it took Lita to take Trip breakfast after he woke.

"Tomorrow," Lita announced when she returned, "that *hombre* gets an electric shaver."

Brenna almost suggested that one of the veterinary fine shavers for animal fur might work, but stopped herself. Lita would only ask why Brenna hadn't trotted one out the first morning she shaved Trip. Brenna didn't want to confess that the obvious hadn't occurred to her because she had been far too eager for any excuse to touch Trip.

Dr. Jamison arrived at eleven and remained sequestered in Trip's room for an hour. The two women were at the reception desk conferring on the afternoon schedule when the tall, silver-haired doctor walked in with his black bag.

"Home seems to agree with him," was Jamison's first amiable comment before he sternly added, "Just don't let him get close to any desk work until he's had more rest. Visitors are okay, but nothing to do with the practice until I say so. Understood?"

Lita raised a dubious eyebrow that silently said doctor's orders would be followed only if Trip Hart himself understood.

"I know," Jamison replied to her unspoken contention. "He's a hard man to keep down."

Brenna almost choked, remembering how truly hard he could be to keep down under certain provocative circumstances.

"A hired nurse will be an expensive proposition," the doctor continued, "unless you two can work together to keep him clean and comfortable. I've arranged for a physical therapist to come over from the next county every other day until he's out of the casts. Then it'll be therapy every weekday for the leg and hand."

Lita and Brenna, both well aware that the cash flow from the practice was good but not *that* good, said in unison, "We can do it."

Jamison nodded his approval. "You've both done a great job so far. His ribs are healing a lot faster than I expected. And what happened to his burns, I'd like to know."

"What burns?" Lita said. "I didn't see any when I sponged him down yesterday."

"That's my point. Where did they go?" He peered over his glasses first at Lita, then at Brenna.

Brenna cleared her throat. "Udder cream." She spread her hands in appeal. "It was all he had in the medicine chest. He made me smear it on."

"Udder cream?" Jamison repeated, wrinkling his nose in disdain.

Brenna nodded. "For chapped udders."

"Udders."

Brenna could see from the roll of Jamison's eyes that the less said, the better. She'd seen that expression on her colleagues' faces in San Jose, and she challenged him with a look that said he was free to explain the inexplicable anytime he liked.

"Placebo effect, no doubt," he muttered. "I'll be back late Friday afternoon." With a wave and a pointed wink at Lita, he was gone.

Like the roll of the eyes, Brenna had also encountered his catchall explanation for what couldn't scientifically be proven. She sighed.

The placebo effect was a medical phenomenon she never experienced in treating animals. M.D.'s, however, had documented it in treating humans. The gist of it was that some patients who believe strongly enough in the healing power of a medicine will show improvement or get well after using it even if the medication contains no active ingredient.

However, letting Jamison believe *that* was infinitely preferable to telling him what she actually feared had happened to the remains of Trip's burns with or without the cream for udders.

The problem with naming the placebo effect as the healer in veterinary medicine was that a colicky horse or cancer-riddled hamster neither believed nor disbelieved in the effectiveness of any medication. With the critical factor of belief ruled out, what then explained either the healing or the cure in the absence of medication?

"What a *zorro argentino* of a hunk," Lita murmured, watching the physician get into his elegant blue sportscar.

"What variety of hunk might that be?" Brenna inquired with a teasing lift of an eyebrow.

Lita gave her a sly grin. "The silver fox variety, *amiga*."

"Ah. Of course."

"Sí," said Lita, following the exit of the sedan with a steady gaze of frank appraisal. "He's a widower, you know. Only five years younger than I am."

"And interested, too. I caught that wink. Why don't you cook dinner for him Friday night?"

Lita tossed her braid over her shoulder with a coquettish flick of her wrist. "I just might. Perhaps I should start trying to match myself up instead of Trip." She gave Brenna a distracted glance. "He still believes I was matchmaking when I hired you, *amiga*. I can tell."

"Really?" Brenna kept a straight face. "He said he apologized."

"He did, but I could see his heart wasn't in it." Lita shook her head in vehement denial and sighed. "In his heart he believes I deliberately stayed away to throw you two together."

"Lita, I don't think he—"

"I know my son," Lita cut in. "It's been worrying me since he came home, but I've thought up a solution."

"What's that?"

"If I move back here for a week or so, he can't suspect me of throwing anyone together. And it will save me driving back and forth if you get night calls. It would solve everything, wouldn't it, *amiga*?"

"Oh—uh, yes." Brenna swallowed back her sudden and complete dismay. "Everything."

"*Muy bien.* It's lunchtime. I'll go home and pack a bag."

9

FROM THE TIME Lita left to pack a bag, to her return with it an hour later, the office phone kept Brenna hopping. She sipped a cup of lukewarm coffee in the moments between calls and reminded herself that Lita had not the foggiest notion of what had almost proceeded to completion over the long weekend. If she had, she'd have stayed away from the ranch during all but office hours.

Brenna thought about Trip, alone in the house. Was he all right? Bored? Needing anything? Without help to tend the phone, she couldn't run in and check up on him.

She wondered if Trip knew of Lita's decision. Had she announced it when she took him his breakfast? What, Brenna wondered, had been his reaction? Had he been dismayed, as she had been, upon hearing the news? Or had he been, perhaps, relieved? She hated to think it.

If only Lita knew what she was obstructing. Brenna, though, couldn't see herself informing Trip's mother that a match had been struck in her absence. Nor could she see herself tiptoeing to Trip's bed at midnight while his mother slept right down the hall.

Perhaps it was all for the best, Brenna told herself. Trip hadn't been wrong in contending that certain matters needed straightening out. The fact also remained that all he had said was that he was falling in love with her. Falling in love was only the first stage, the easiest to back out of. The easiest for a man to talk himself out of. Head over heels, as she herself had fallen so fast, was not something she could expect of Trip this soon. His second thoughts were proof enough of that.

The fact also remained that she had tumbled head over heels for a man she knew a great deal about before she had even met him. Now that she knew more, her love for him had grown. What she had revealed of herself to Trip, however, was incomplete. Yet, how could she disclose that strange and alarming aspect of herself to him without risking more than she could afford to lose? Hadn't she already put herself on the line at the clinic and been blackballed?

Trip, like Dr. Jamison, was a scientific realist. In working with his files, Brenna had read his methodical observations and deductive diagnoses, noted his prudent prescriptives. On only the rarest of occasions had he followed a gut feeling and done solely what "felt" right. In short, he was an excellent vet who put his trust in proven medical methods and almost never gambled with an animal's health or life.

But there was little time for Brenna to ponder how or when to unveil her deep, dark secret. Lita's return and the arrival of the first afternoon appointment were simultaneous, forcing Brenna's thoughts and attention back to keeping Trip's practice on a steady course.

"YOU'RE WHAT?" Trip said, blinking in disbelief at Lita, who stood in his doorway with her suitcase a little later that afternoon.

"Moving in for a week or so," Lita repeated, "to help out with things."

Madre, Trip thought, shutting his eyes to hide his reaction. When he opened them a moment later, he had to force himself not to roll them in dismay.

"Hey," he said, and faked a smile, "great."

Lita gestured down the hall. "I'll take the room next to Brenna's and bring you lunch after I unpack."

"Thanks." He watched his smiling mother leave and then sank back into his pillows to curse his fate and wonder if Brenna was cursing hers. Or blessing it, maybe? He couldn't help wondering if she'd had a second thought or two about getting creative with him.

He had to wonder until well into the next day, as two emergency operations kept Brenna in surgery until almost midnight. By the time she finished, he was asleep. She was back in the office before he woke the next morning.

Trip didn't see her until after Conrad Metz came and went. The husky physical therapist had blond hair, blue eyes and a physique worthy of a wrestler, which it turned out he was in his spare time. Trip found himself relieved that Brenna was busy. The dichotomy between his own deficiencies and Conrad's splendid wholeness was too great. Trip's only consolation was that the handsome therapist was happily married and had three small children.

It was after Conrad had departed that Brenna emerged from the office for a quick lunch in Trip's room with him and Lita.

"How'd therapy go?" she inquired, keeping her eyes off Trip and on the burrito on her plate. The last thing she wanted was for Lita to suspect a thing. There were complications enough as it was.

"Not bad. He's got me working weights with the good arm and leg. Sit-ups are right around the corner."

"Now, Trip. Conrad said no sit-ups for several weeks," Lita corrected.

"As if there's any danger that I could attempt one too soon even if I wanted to," Trip drawled with a glance at Brenna.

Lita fixed him with a motherly gaze of reproof. "You checked out of the hospital too soon. I don't put anything past you after that, *hombre*."

"Checking out was my last insubordination. Relax."

"I'll relax the day you're back on your feet."

"Foot," Trip reminded her.

"You still have two and that makes feet, whether they both hold you up or not," Lita contended, rising from her chair. "Who wants a nice juicy peach for dessert?"

Trip waved a hand. "Pass. I'm full."

Biting into the last of her burrito, Brenna gave a negative shake of her head.

Lita went off to the kitchen, calling, "Byron! Malia! Where are my favorite *poquitos*? I have a nice juicy surprise for you."

"That's my mother—full of juicy surprises," Trip quipped, then turned to Brenna with a sobered gaze. "You're quiet today. Rough night?"

She nodded. "I lost Old Gold in surgery last night."

"Luella Mangione's golden retriever? What happened?"

"He lost an argument with a wild boar."

"Jeez," Trip said with a wince. "How's Luella taking it?"

"She's grief stricken."

Trip blew out a harsh breath. "Poor Luella. She can't have children. Old Gold was like a kid to her. She brought him in to me every time he sneezed." He shook his head. "I'll give her a call later this afternoon—despite doctor's orders to keep my nose out of my own business."

"She'd like that," Brenna said with a grateful smile. "She thinks so much of you, like everyone else does around here."

"They'll think less when they see what's left of me," he muttered.

"Several people called today asking how you are."

"What did you say?"

"The same thing Lita says. That you're home, but not quite ready for visitors yet."

"Good. I don't want to face anyone until I have to."

"Dr. Jamison did say visitors are okay," Brenna pointed out gently.

"Jamison," Trip snorted. "I can have company day and night, but can't poke around my own client affairs and account books if I want to. What medical logic is there in that, I'd like to know?"

"None," Brenna said. "I happen to think he's wrong to order you not to work. It's a good sign that you want to be involved again in the practice."

"Yeah." Trip smiled, but it was rueful. "A good sign. I keep forgetting I'm going to have to sell out. What's the use?"

"Trip, your practice needs you for the time being, at least, and so do I."

He gave her a piercing glance. "I thought you were doing my job perfectly well without me."

"Does it bother you to think that?"

"Yes," he admitted after hesitating a moment. "This practice is my baby. All mine. I don't like the idea of anyone filling my shoes as easily and quickly as my mother says you've done."

"She says that because she doesn't want you to worry about a thing. To be honest, I'm barely keeping my head above water a lot of the time."

"It doesn't show."

"Wait until you review my work to judge that. My point is that the briefing you gave me on Trixie saved a lot of diagnostic work once I got to her. And there's no telling if Old Gold might have survived with two vets instead of one in surgery last night."

"One and a half, you mean," Trip scoffed. "Let's not pretend I can do surgery."

Brenna shrugged. "You could have assisted. I'll bet you could handle a partial prep and administer anesthesia right now if necessary."

Trip's silence in the moments that followed told Brenna she'd struck a live, if carefully buried nerve.

"I could have used your advice, too, last night," she added, to drive home the point. "Experience counts. You've been practicing twice as long as I have."

"I've been doing a few other things longer than you have, too," he replied, his tone now clipped and curt. "One of them is lurching around on a crutch. Another is making a bloody mess of my face with a safety razor. Another is wondering . . ."

"What?"

"I—nothing."

Brenna watched a ruddy flush creep up his neck.

"You're having second thoughts, aren't you?" she guessed. "About us."

"Hell, yes, I'm thinking twice," he gruffly admitted. "Aren't *you*?"

"No. I'm only hoping Lita leaves before your negative thoughts get the *best* of you."

WHAT TRIP LOST before Lita left was his no-visitors policy. Once word circulated through the community that he was home, there was no stopping the stream of phone calls from friends and clients wanting to visit him.

It was Lita who finally marched in and told him he would either take personal calls and receive visitors or hire expensive office help to handle the phone overload. His first visitor arrived thirty minutes later.

Bearing flowers, cookies, candy, fruit baskets and potted plants, Trip's friends and clients came, a steady stream of sympathetic well-wishers. Children whose pets Trip had treated brought bright helium balloons to be tied to his bedposts and decorated his casts with happy faces and childish scrawls. Trip's sisters came, too— Elena for a whole day with her husband and children, and Bianca for two days all the way from New Mexico. Conrad Metz had to herd people out for Trip's therapy sessions.

"Jamison will kill me. When he said visitors, he didn't mean a crowd," Lita fretted, both frustrated and pleased by the overwhelming response from far and wide.

"The more there are, the better Trip looks," Brenna assured her. Indeed, he looked happier as the week passed. His dark moods grew shorter and brighter. Most important, Brenna noted, he stopped referring to himself as a cripple, even kiddingly. She wondered if he had stopped thinking of himself as one, too. She couldn't tell, for her time with him all week was limited and always shared by someone else.

Byron and Malia and the Dwarves, of course, had an absolute ball holding court on Trip's bed.

By the time Dr. Jamison returned on Friday afternoon, it seemed to Brenna that the entire population of the county had trekked through the old ranch house to Trip's room for a visit.

Jamison said it best. "Did I say the world could drop in?" he wryly inquired, eyeing the signatures and playful doodles that covered Trip's plaster casts. After dismissing Brenna and Lita to examine Trip at length, the doctor came out to the kitchen where the two women were having an iced-tea break.

"How would you like to trade tea for cocktails at your place and dinner in town?" the silver fox inquired of Lita.

Lita almost dropped her glass before blushing and then turning to Brenna. "Why... what do you think, *amiga*? Can you manage without me tonight?"

"Go," Brenna said, mentally blessing the good doctor for possessing the charm and good looks to turn Lita to mush. "You've been here around the clock too long. It's Friday. Go home for the weekend."

"But you, *muchacha*. You need time off, too. And Trip needs—"

Brenna waved her down. "Go. Have fun. I'll play nurse. I'll even unplug the phone and take a breather myself if you'll feel better about it."

"*Muy bien*," Lita decided, her eyes dancing. "I'll go pack my things and tell Trip."

Brenna chitchatted amiably with Jamison until Lita came back with her suitcase and lamented, "He's asleep, *amiga*. I didn't wake him."

"I'll follow you home, *señora*," Jamison said to Lita, taking her suitcase and leading her away.

Brenna activated the phone answering machine before their two cars reached the road. She scribbled "The doctors are out" on a square of cardboard and hung it on the mailbox to halt the flow of drop-ins. She put Byron and Malia in the dog run. Finally she looked down at what she was wearing and made a face at her jeans and green scrub shirt. Not quite what the doctor might order for a man having second thoughts.

Nor would she wear anything that wouldn't slip off with the greatest of ease, she reflected moments later as she stared at her flushed face in the mirror before she stepped into a cool shower.

Having never planned or executed the deliberate seduction of a man before, she felt apprehensive. And excited.

She would make fettuccine Alfredo for dinner, she decided, and a butter-lettuce salad with mustard vinaigrette. The gift bottle of wine someone had left during the week would be perfect, as Trip's gift chocolates would be for dessert.

After showering, she slipped into a silky yellow shift that zipped up the front. No buttons, no snaps, no bra, no hose, no panties. She shimmied her shoulders in a delicious shiver, thinking of how effortlessly Trip could strip her bare later with one hand alone.

There was still the problem of what she hadn't told him, of course. But she pushed it out of her mind as she brushed and blow-dried her hair. Later, she told herself. After he fell head over heels. After he came to love her enough to keep an open mind, she would tell him. Tonight was for loving, not confessing.

Simmering with inner bubbles of anticipation, she headed for the kitchen to start dinner, then peeked into Trip's room. Golden light and sunset shadow washed the walls and his motionless form on the bed. The gilded air was warm, laced with the scent of the get-well flowers massed on every available surface. Brenna breathed deeply of the fragrant air and held it in her lungs as the man in the bed stirred, opened his eyes and focused on her in the doorway.

"Brenna?" Trip's murmur was thick, honeyed with sleep.

"Hi," she replied on a tremulous outbreath, then said in a rush, "Lita's gone home for the night—and out to dinner with Doc Jamison."

"Home for the . . ." He blinked the sleep from his eyes and stared at her. "We're alone?"

She nodded and came to the side of the bed. "Until tomorrow."

He blinked again.

"Take your time waking up," she added, seeing that her good news would take a few quiet moments to sink in. "The fettuccine still needs me in the kitchen."

A little later she brought him a glass of Soave and found his bed empty, his bathroom door closed. From behind it she heard the gurgle of water filling the washbasin. Leaving his wine on the nightstand, Brenna went back to the kitchen.

After pacing the linoleum floor for what seemed an eternity, she returned with her own wineglass in hand and found Trip with his shoulders propped against his pillows and the sheet pulled to his waist.

"Is it dinner yet?" he inquired without lifting his gaze from the glass in his hand.

"It's ready whenever we are."

He looked up and gestured with his glass for her to come in. "How about a toast? I hate to drink alone."

"So do I." Brenna sat on the mattress beside him and touched her glass to his. "What's the toast?"

Trip smiled slightly. "To Everett Jamison, M.D. A man who knows a *señora bellíssima* when he sees one."

"And to Carmelita Hart," Brenna rejoined, "who knows a *zorro argentino* at first sight."

They laughed together and enjoyed their wine while Brenna told Trip about her week, the ups and downs, the way foxy Jamison had winked at Lita that day in the office.

Trip yearningly watched her lips form words, smooth into a smile, pucker when she frowned. She was lovely, he thought as he listened and gazed at her. And so very much a woman. Too much woman to waste herself as she seemed to have every intention of doing with him.

"What . . . ?"

Trip read in Brenna's soft query and raised eyebrows how far his thoughts had wandered. "Sorry, I . . . was just thinking."

"Second thoughts again, by chance?" Brenna asked after a long pause stretched too thin to support the weight of their collective silence.

Trip nodded, drained his glass and set it aside. "They've been multiplying in my head all week," he said. "It won't work."

Brenna set her glass next to his. "What won't work?"

"This thing between us."

"Why not?"

"You deserve a man who can sweep you away. A month ago I could have done it, but I'm not that man today."

"A man like Rhett Butler, you mean, who swept Scarlett O'Hara off her feet and carried her up the stairway to the untold pleasures of his bed?"

"Precisely." Trip turned his dark-hot gaze unflinchingly on her. "That's what I'd do with you if I could. Every night without fail. But I can't."

"No, you don't have a stairway handy," Brenna agreed, her determined gaze as unwavering as his.

"You could have any man you want, Brenna."

"You're the man I want," she said, her tone and eyes softening as she touched a finger to his angular jaw. "Not just your body. You. Don't you want me that way, too?"

Trip caught Brenna's wrist in his hand. "You know the answer to that," he said fiercely, "but what I want and what I can do about it are worlds apart. I'm almost flat on my back. I'm stuck there."

"I know that. I've known it from the start. I have no romantic illusions about what you can and can't do right now. It doesn't keep me from wanting you right now. *Right this minute*. I'm ready, Trip. Are you?"

Trip closed his eyes and pressed her hand to his chest. "A month ago I'd have been the one asking *you* that."

"I'd have said yes without thinking twice."

He opened his eyes. "You'd have also been the one flat on your back—for a far different reason. I'd have given you everything." He smoothed his hand from her wrist to her elbow and repeated in a velvet whisper, "Everything."

"Give me what you can tonight and I'll be more than satisfied."

"I have no idea what I can give anymore."

"Don't underestimate yourself." Brenna feathered the fingers of her free hand through Trip's hair and let them trace the whorl of his ear.

"I can't help it. I've never been on ground this shaky in bed before, Brenna."

"Neither have I. I was always flat on my back before, for the most part."

"And enjoying it, I hope."

"Not as much as I'm going to enjoy tonight."

"Don't count on a whole lot. I'm in foreign territory at the moment."

"Then you'll just have to feel your way, won't you?" whispered Brenna. She kicked her sandals off, stretched out on the bed next to Trip and touched her lips to his. "Don't worry. I take the Pill. I'm protected."

He moaned and gave her his mouth. A moment later Brenna knew they wouldn't be ready for dinner for a very long time, if ever. It was a good thing she had turned off every kitchen burner. Any last thoughts plaguing Trip's mind were clearly departing. His arm was curled around her, holding her tight, molding her upper body to his.

Trip's senses reeled. He felt the stiff points of Brenna's nipples against his chest, the hungry dart of her tongue in his mouth, the weight of her leg as she slipped it over his cast and gently lowered it.

"Whatever happens, I do love you, *corazón*," he whispered against her lips. "I hope that's enough."

"*Corazón*," she repeated wonderingly, the word sweet and strange on her tongue. "Meaning?"

"Sweetheart. Loved one."

"Loved one? Oh, Trip. Just the way you say it turns me on. Don't stop saying it."

Trip repeated the endearment between the open-mouthed kisses he pressed to her throat. He whispered it in tandem with the soft whir of her zipper when he lowered it and freed her breasts to his seeking touch. Brenna's dusky rose nipples stood taut. Her skin was firm and hot.

She sat up and let the top of her silky shift pool around her waist. Reaching out, she flicked the bedside lamp on. Its golden glow burnished her bare breasts and softened the evening shadows in the room.

"How did you know I like the light on?" murmured Trip, his eyes drawn to where his hand claimed one breast.

"I didn't. It's for me. I don't want to miss one perfect detail tonight."

"You're the perfect detail, *corazón*."

"Freckles aren't perfect."

Trip's gaze trailed the trace of his fingers over the lush curves of her breasts. "On you they are. If I could, I'd count every one of them from top to bottom, front to back." His dimple deepened. "With my tongue."

Brenna trembled at the thought and the erotic image it evoked. "Start with one and take your time," she prompted. With a provocative arch of her spine, she moved to let his seeking tongue taste and his fingers touch.

"Oh, yes," came his hot whisper between her breasts when she pressed her thumbs to his nipples and rubbed.

Then he was doing the same to her with his teeth and lips and fingertips. His tongue laved her with such captivating finesse that her breath came too hard and fast to sustain without ceasing entirely. She pulled away with a gasp.

Trip, panting just as hard as she, let her go. "I hurt you?"

"No . . . oh, no . . ."

"What, then?"

She curved her hand to his where he cupped her left breast. "Trip, when you kiss, you turn me inside out. You make me feel so good I can't breathe."

"That good?" But he knew fully how good, for Brenna's breasts were swollen and flushed from the rasp of his teeth and tongue, her nipples as round and hard as pearls. She was aroused and couldn't conceal her desire from him. He knew, too, how great was his own need. Too far gone now for second thoughts.

"That good," Brenna confirmed, drawing back to look at him and try to catch her breath. There was no hope of breathing normally, though, once her gaze crossed the edge of the sheet at his waist. Only then did she realize he was wearing nothing but his two plaster casts. Under the sheet, he was ready. Hugely, gloriously ready.

She caught her lower lip between her teeth and forced her eyes back to meet his. His, however, were riveted on the hemline of her shift where it skimmed her upper thighs. As if drawn to join his gaze, his hand grazed down from her breasts and slipped beneath the silky material.

He licked his lips. "Is this all you've got on?"

"Not for long," was Brenna's whispered reply.

She rose from the bed to let her shift fall past her waist and down her legs to the floor. There was no time for shyness when she paused and invited Trip's intent gaze, for in that same moment, he flung the sheet aside and made her everlastingly grateful that she wasn't blind.

She was beautiful, Trip marveled, watching her move to the foot of the bed. With eyes the amber of fine sherry, her tiny freckles punctuating the deep flush of her cheeks, she was the loveliest creature he'd ever seen, the essence of femininity from her delicious rose-tipped breasts to the nest of pale brown curls at the juncture of her thighs.

He saw in her eyes the glow of what she intended as she knelt in the narrow space between his cast and his leg.

"Brenna—"

"No thinking, Trip." She settled on her calves and trailed the fingers of one hand from his bare ankles to his knee.

Unable to so much as form a thought after that, Trip watched her fingertips riffle the hair on his leg. Watched her flatten both palms on the surface of his thigh and smooth them up, then back down, then up again until he was holding his breath for her to move higher.

"You're a beautiful man, Trip Hart," she whispered, sweeping her lashes up and meeting the dark heat in his eyes. "Michelangelo's *David* is a wimp compared to you."

"He wasn't looking at what I'm looking at when Mike carved him," was Trip's husky reply.

"Ah, so I'm to blame for this flagrant display of manly interest?"

"Entirely."

"That's the nicest compliment I've ever been paid," she murmured, gently cupping her palm to the twin spheres of heavy, quiescent flesh nested in the hair that grew dark and dense where his thighs joined. She squeezed slightly, then slid her palm up to where he swelled, long and thick and incredibly hard.

Trip's lips parted, his eyes fell shut. "Brenna," he gasped, "I'm not—" He hesitated. "It's been a long time since I've been with anyone."

"Me, too."

"I don't want to disappoint you."

"I have a feeling you won't."

"If you keep doing that, I will."

"Just tell me when to stop. In the meantime, how does this feel?" She placed her palms flat on the mattress at either side of his hips and lowered herself to tantalize him with the tips of her breasts.

His soft moan and the tug of his fingers in her hair were his only replies to how extraordinarily good it felt to him. She only wished she could fully convey how perfect, how right it felt to her, too. Words were one way. And there was a second—the intimate, loving way Brenna chose.

Cradling him in her hands, she pressed wet, open kisses up and down the rigid underside of his sex, drew him deep into her mouth and stroked him with her swirling tongue until he throbbed. Never had she felt so womanly, so powerful, so filled to overflowing with the desire to please the man she loved.

"Brenna . . ." Trip touched her cheek with a forefinger that trembled. "You don't have to do this for me."

She drew away and blew softly on him. "I *want* to. I love doing this for you and to you. All the way if you like."

"I'm not saying I wouldn't like it. I'm thinking of you."

Brenna curled her fingers where her lips had been and treasured him. "You'd take *me* over if the tables were turned. And you'd love doing it as much as I'm loving this."

"You don't know half of what I'd do if I could," he murmured.

"Oh, I'm sure I do," she insisted softly. "I've been paying close attention. As men go, you aren't a leg man or a tush man. Or even a breast man, past a certain point. You'd want to spend a long time knowing me this way."

This, Trip couldn't deny. Brenna had his number, but good. The most intimate aspects of the female body intrigued and fascinated him. He took a special, unabashed pleasure in giving that way. And he could see from the glow in her eyes that Brenna welcomed that fact in a way that his ethereal, sex-shy ex-wife had never begun to even approach when he was married.

He couldn't help asking, "How do you know I'm like that?"

"Your mouth. The way you move it when you kiss me." Brenna gave him a slow, provocative smile and traced a finger around the velvety tip of his manhood. "It gives you away. I knew from the first kiss why you've been staring at the ceiling thinking you'll never be able to hold your own with me in bed."

She knew that much about him, did she? Trip couldn't decide whether to be pleased beyond measure by her acute perception of his sexual preferences, or chagrined that he'd been so easily read. In either case, he couldn't argue with a woman who looked so happy that he'd be eager and avid to bring her to peak upon peak with his mouth alone—under normal circumstances. But there was the rub. Circumstances were far from normal this night.

"Now that you know, can you blame me for missing what I'm missing?" he murmured in an uneven whisper.

"No, but I *can* blame you for thinking you have to miss anything with me. You only have to miss being in total control of the situation tonight."

"Do you know what you're saying?"

Brenna nodded. "I'm ready to be as up close and personal with you as you are right now with me." She searched his face. "Does that shock you?"

He slowly shook his head. "It amazes me. You amaze me."

Brenna set her fingertips to tracing again. "Your comfort level is mine, Trip. I want everything you can give, too. I just didn't know how to say it without sounding—well, indelicate."

Trip lifted her hand from him and tugged. "Come here, *corazón*. There's only one way *I* know to say what I feel without sounding a hell of a lot more than indelicate."

"Tell me exactly what you want, Trip. I don't want to hurt your ribs."

He raised his arm cast upright and drew her forward. "Over my chest," he prompted. "With all your weight on your knees."

Placing a knee on either side of him, she straightened and looked down at him. Then, very slowly, she lifted one leg and placed the ball of her foot where her knee had rested.

She knew her pose was indelicate but she didn't care. There was nothing delicate about the injuries Trip had suffered. Special situations called for special measures. Beyond that, she felt thrilled to offer herself in such an open way to a man who so clearly appreciated every nuance of what she was offering.

Indelicate, indeed, she thought, looking down into his face. Trip was regarding her as if she were the most feminine, most beautiful, most precious of women.

She saw the pulse in his throat throb fast beneath his skin, saw his eyes fasten on his destination as he stroked a warm, unerring downward swatch from the cleavage of her breasts to her belly and beyond.

"You," he whispered as his fingers treasured her thighs, "are so beautiful. I can't believe I'm doing this." He rubbed the backs of his knuckles against her crisp curls. "And this..." He slipped his hand, palm-up between her legs and cherished her. "And this..." He stroked the length of his middle finger to her, parted her petaled flesh, sought out and found that wild, sensitive spot that made her rock her pelvis forward and swing her knee out to invite more of his intimate caress.

"Ah, Trip...yes, anything you want...I want it, too...."

One finger, then two slipped up into her, stoking a fire that radiated unbearable heat through her every pore. Brenna trembled and sighed with delight. Long moments later, she gasped with even greater joy when he cupped her bottom, lifted his head and pressed his hot mouth to her. Only then did she fully realize how consummate a master of the art he was, how avid and able to please. He knew just how to excite, where to probe, when to linger, when to withdraw and just breathe on her. Stroking fast, slow, hard, whisper light, he made her moan and pant and melt until she was just this side of total bliss.

Her meltdown, however, wasn't preparation enough for the searing moment that stopped her runaway heart when Trip pressed her down onto the fullness of his erection.

They stared at each other, almost in shock, once he was sheathed to the hilt in her slick heat. Then Brenna began to move, setting a gentle rhythm intended to spare him pain. When she had imagined making love with Trip, she had anticipated the necessity of moving like this once they were united. What she hadn't imagined was that taking care not to jar him would have its own erotic rewards in building their mutual pleasure so slowly to its peak.

Wishing that Brenna could ride him with wild abandon and take everything she needed, Trip slipped his hand to where they were joined and stroked her where she was most sensitive until he felt her inner muscles pulse and coil to the highest plateau around him.

"Take it, *corazón*," he urged, increasing the sweet friction until she tensed and then shuddered into the longest, most sensational orgasm of her life.

She was misty with tears of joy and still pulsing around him in the ebb of release when she bowed down and whispered into his mouth, "You make me love you so much. Come, my love . . . come in me . . . ."

With a low groan, Trip gave himself wholly to her inner clasp, sank his fingers into the undulating curve of her derriere and erupted in a violent spate of volcanic bursts that shook him heart and soul from the primal roots of his being.

When he could breathe again, see, hear, think again, he reached up and brushed Brenna's tears from her eyelashes with fingers that shook from the force of an emotion that knew no name.

Never had he loved a woman like this. Never had he been loved like this. Never in his entire life had he felt so complete and whole.

10

BRENNA AND TRIP REMAINED one for a long time after their last tremors of fulfillment had subsided to soft sighs, murmurs and incoherent whispers of praise and love for each other.

They couldn't stop smiling. Or gazing at each other in wonder. Or reaching out to gently touch and touch and touch again.

Afterplay. The tender kisses on fingertips. The languid sweep of a warm palm along an inner thigh. The cherishing cup of a hand to a hip, a shoulder, a breast, a rounded knee. The loving trace of a finger on an eyebrow, a profile, a dimple.

"I'll never forget tonight," Trip whispered, "or the way you look right now."

Brenna nodded. "I've never known a first time like this."

"I'm already wanting more. I can feel it."

"I'm rising, too. Is this what they call 'chemistry'?"

"Must be. I could stay inside you forever." His dimple deepened. "Or at least all night."

"Stay. Now and all night and longer. I need you."

"I need you, too, *corazón*. More than you know."

"I'm yours."

"Not as completely as you'll be after I get out of these casts. I promise."

"Trip, there's no need for promises. You gave me the greatest pleasure of my life tonight."

He pressed her fingertips to his lips. "And you gave me mine. But imagine the love we'll make the day I can move on you as well as in you. When I look down into your beautiful eyes as well as up to them. When I give you my weight as well as take yours."

"I'm imagining," she assured him.

"Yes, imagine," he urged, his eyes heating with each word. "I'll press you into the bed and feel your legs wrap around me and watch you come under me. I'll—" He sucked in a breath as Brenna's inner muscles gloved his hardening sex.

"What else?" came Brenna's silky whisper. "Tell me. Everything."

"I'll . . . oh, honey . . . keep doing that."

"Only if you'll keep talking."

"I'll spread you out on the bed . . ."

Brenna closed her eyes and let the ravishing images form. "Mmm."

"And I'll suck little love-marks . . ."

She cupped her breasts together so that Trip's fingers could circle both nipples at once. "Where?"

"On the insides of your thighs . . . where only I can see them."

She opened her eyes and watched the supple motion of his thumb and fingertips on her. "And then?"

"I'll tease you until you beg."

"For what?"

"My tongue."

"Promise?"

"I never make promises I don't keep."

"I'll remember that . . . when the casts come off. . . ."

ALL BRENNA COULD REMEMBER as she showered and dressed for work the next morning was that Trip was everything, but *everything*, she had ever wanted in a man. She had never felt so treasured and loved and desired as she felt with him. She had never experienced with any man the sexual satisfaction she had known with him. And she had never loved a man with such joyful, shameless abandon as she had loved Trip in their long night together.

Office hours on Saturdays ran from ten in the morning to two in the afternoon. Lita called in at nine.

"*Buenos días, muchacha.* How is today doing without me?"

"Fine." Brenna blushed. *Marvelous. Fantastic. Magnificent. Thank you from the bottom of my socks for bringing Tristan Perez Hart into the world.* "Trip's still asleep."

"*Bueno.* Sleep heals. Listen, I won't be back until Monday, if you can live with that."

"No problem," Brenna said, renewed anticipation oozing from every pore at the knowledge that tonight and tomorrow night, too, would be hers and Trip's alone. "Did you have fun with the fox?"

"*Sí, señorita. Fantastico.* I'm cooking him *chilies rellenos* and *flan* tonight at my place. What do you think of that?"

"I'd say he's driving more than a mile or two for dinner tonight. He must be crazy about you."

"*Amiga*, the man is a *quicksilver* fox. He takes my breath away."

Brenna smiled. "Is love in bloom?"

"I'll tell you on Monday. Until then, keep Trip's visitors to as few as you can. He needs his rest after last week."

He needs more than you think after last night. "I'll try."

"*Gracias, muchacha.* What would I do without you? You're like a daughter to me. If only Trip would . . ." Lita sighed. "I'm at home if you need me. Give Trip my love."

"I will." *And mine, too.*

"Tripito," Lita said to him on Monday morning, "you look like a new man."

"I had a decent weekend," Trip replied, keeping a perfectly straight face. "How was yours?"

"*Maravilloso.*" Lita's eyes went dreamy. "Everett is a lovely man."

Trip grinned. "Everett, eh? Things must be getting cozy."

"*Sí.*" Lita's dreamy gaze shifted to focus on her son again. "How does the idea of having a *padrasto* strike you?"

"A stepfather? You mean—"

Lita nodded. "He put two hundred miles round trip on his car to have dinner with me Saturday night. I put the same on mine to spend yesterday with him. We talked on the phone this morning, and he's going to call tonight. After he sees you on Wednesday, he's taking me to the movies. What do you think, *niño*?"

Trip winked. "Go to a drive-in. Steam up the car windows."

"It strikes you right?"

"I can't think of a *padrasto* I'd like better than Everett Jamison. Has he proposed?"

"Almost. I'll say yes when he does. I know it's sudden, but I married your father one month after I met him and couldn't have been happier. Everett and his wife fell in love at first sight and never fell out. We are not two people who can stand still when lightning strikes."

"Why do I get the sinking feeling that I'm going to lose my receptionist?"

"Because it only makes good sense for Everett to live in San Luis where he works. He has a wonderful house, perfect for two. We'll keep my adobe for getaways and vacations. I'll find you a receptionist, Trip. Don't worry."

"I'm not worried. I'm happy for you, *mamacita*. You've been alone too long."

"So have you," Lita said, and then waved a hand to dismiss the scowl she anticipated from him. "I know. I should mind my own business. Well, I will from now on. With Everett."

Trip gave her a sidelong glance. "Is he calling you at home tonight?"

"No. I told him I'd be here."

"Oh." Trip tried not to look disappointed. "You're moving back in, then?"

"Yes, and moving back out for Wednesday night for obvious reasons." She gave Trip a foxy wink of her own and rose from her chair. "Now, then. I see Brenna has already brought you breakfast. What else can I do for you before I go to work?"

Trip looked directly into his mother's eyes. "How about moving home for good tonight instead of Wednesday? No offense."

"But—*why, niño*?"

"How does the idea of a *nuera* strike you?"

Very slowly Lita sat back down in the chair she had vacated. "A daughter-in-law? What . . . who?"

"B. J. Deveney."

"Brenna? *Madre Maria*," Lita whispered, her eyes fluttering in disbelief before they misted with sudden, happy tears. "Why didn't I notice?"

"It strikes you right?"

"*Sí*. A thousand times *sí*. You've already—" she gulped "—proposed?"

Trip held up a hand. "I haven't said a word. I haven't even thought it through. I only mentioned it because you shouldn't think I'm kicking you out just so I can have a cheap fling with my relief vet. That's not what we're having. It's serious. ¿*Comprende?*"

"*Comprend.* Two beds are always too many for two people in love—" she arched her brows meaningfully "—whether the lovers are in their thirties or sixties."

"I begin to see why you didn't notice a thing last week when I was sure you'd see my heart on my sleeve."

Lita shrugged and smiled. "Love is blind. All I could think about was the way Everett winked at me. I felt like a schoolgirl again."

"Some matchmaker *you've* turned out to be," Trip teased.

"You can't say I didn't do one thing right."

"What?"

"I hired Brenna!" crowed Lita, giving her dearest and only son a mother-bear hug and a huge, smacking kiss on each cheek.

IT WAS LATE on Wednesday afternoon, after Everett and Lita left together, that Brenna brought Trip a stack of patient files to review in bed.

"What Jamison doesn't know won't hurt him," Brenna said. "These are in chronological order from my first day here. You should know what I've been doing."

An hour later she came back with dinner on a tray, compliments of Lita. It was *arroz con pollo*, better known as chicken with rice.

"Lita is the best cook I've ever known."

Trip looked up from the file he was reviewing. "Her motto is *panza lleno, corazón contento.*"

"In other words?"

"Full stomach, contented heart."

"I don't wonder that Everett Jamison looks like one immensely happy man these days."

Trip set the file aside. "He isn't the only man these days with a happy heart."

"Mine's wearing a big smile, too."

"Mmm. It's wearing more than that. Think you can find a spot other than my lap for that tray for the next hour or so?"

"I might be able to." She gave him a slow, knowing smile. "Why?"

"Because something besides my heart is happy to see you right now, *corazón*. You shouldn't wear short-shorts when you serve dinner."

Brenna set the tray down on the dresser. "It's summer," she murmured. "It's hot. *I'm* hot. Even shorts are hot on a night like this." She slid her fingers into her elastic waistband and peeled it down an inch.

"You wore them on purpose."

"Just for you." She peeled them down another inch. And I'll take them off for the same reason."

"Come here. I'll help you. After that, you can help with mine."

She did. And he did. And she did. And dinner was a very late affair, indeed.

"YOU KNOW WHAT YOU FORGOT to bill Ash Pemberton for?" Trip said after dinner when he had resumed reviewing the files and Brenna was sipping a glass of sherry and scanning a vet journal next to him.

"What?"

"Trixie's injection."

"She didn't need one." *Not now. Please not now,* she thought, her fingers tightening on her glass. *Now is the wrong time. Later.*

Trip furrowed his brow at her. "She always needs a shot to calm down."

"It took some talking," Brenna said with an attempt at a nonchalant shrug, "but she settled down without one."

Trip was silent for a minute before he closed the file. "You're sure you didn't just forget to bill it?"

"Positive. I had the best billing records out of all the vets at the San Jose clinic."

"That's another thing on my mind." Trip frowned and tapped the stack of files. "I fully agree with every course of treatment you've prescribed here. You've done nothing but practice good medicine. What made those guys think you were too progressive?"

"You know how men can be in this profession," Brenna evaded. "Sometimes just being a woman is being too progressive. I've met with my share of resistance on that count from my first day of vet school."

"How many women in your class?"

"You're looking at her."

"There were none in mine."

Brenna passed her glass under his nose in hope that the heady bouquet would distract him further. "Want to finish this for me while I clean up in the kitchen?"

"Sure. I still don't get it, though. You'd have had *my* vote for partner and I'm a conservative guy."

He took her glass, but Brenna saw a shadow linger between his brows.

In the kitchen she accidentally broke a plate and stood staring at the shards of it in the sink. Nothing unusual had happened since Trixie. Nothing had stepped in to save Old Gold. For all she knew, the power was gone, never to manifest again.

"Until you learn its ways, dear," Howmedica had once said, "it can be most unpredictable. I went a whole year without a peep from it after it first moved in me. It kept at me after that lull until I had to pay attention and start studying with an experienced healer. It helps enormously if you learn to meditate. When you decide to pay attention, dear, ring me up."

Maybe this was no temporary lull, Brenna told herself. Maybe it was gone for good.

BY THE END OF ANOTHER WEEK, Trip's ribs had healed enough that a sneeze or a cough or a laugh caused less actual pain than discomfort. Capable of more flexible movement, he became increasingly agile on his crutch and ranged unassisted around the house and yard.

Sprawled in a chair, with his leg cast propped on the seat of a chair facing him, he sat in the kitchen morning and evening and kept Brenna company while she cooked. To their great surprise they found this utilitarian room well designed for both erotic and sensual pursuit. It was far better equipped and furnished for a disabled man and his lover to make love in than the bedroom was.

After several glorious trysts in the kitchen, Brenna knew she would never look at a kitchen chair or table or counter in quite the same way again. With Trip able to bend at the waist, the rest of the house, too, began to teem with creative possibilities that two lovers could eagerly and breathlessly seek out and test one by one.

Trip's therapy with Conrad strengthened his good arm and leg. He religiously exercised his able hand and began to use it with greater dexterity in eating, shaving and even helping in the kitchen—in ways more than just culinary.

The day he did his first real sit-up in therapy, Brenna arched an eyebrow at him afterward and inquired, "How would you like to do something we haven't done together before?"

Trip's roguish, unequivocal reply was, "There's *nothing* we haven't done except what we can't do until the casts come off."

"Oh, yes there is."

"What?"

"Field calls. I have three this afternoon. Come with me."

"Brenna . . ."

"If nothing else, you'll be out and about. You could use a change of scene, couldn't you?"

"Sure, but—"

"At least come along for the ride. The first stop is Tony Montoya's place."

"What's wrong out there?"

Brenna could tell from the way his eyes lit when he asked the question that he couldn't help being strongly interested. She could also see his equally strong hesitation to ease back into matters he might be forced to abandon altogether in the not-too-distant future.

"A couple of his milk cows have mastitis," she replied, her expression grim. Infected udders in a dairy herd were no laughing matter. Widespread infection could shut the milk production of a herd down to a trickle, and treatment could be expensive.

"Damn." Trip brought his fist down hard on the kitchen table. "His herd's been mastitis free for three years. It took me over a year to get it that way. I told him he was asking for trouble when he hired that new milker with the hard-luck story. Tony's a soft touch. The guy's a slouch who takes shortcuts when Tony isn't breathing down his neck."

"I'd say you need to have a few more words with Tony about his hired help," Brenna observed.

"More than a few, from the sound of it."

"You've seen ten times as much bovine mastitis as I have," Brenna prompted, "and you know Tony's herd and milking setup inside out."

Trip was silent for several moments, thinking. Finally he shrugged and said, "Might as well, I guess. It's been a while since I shot the breeze with Tony."

"*Muy bien.*" Brenna stood and briskly rubbed her hands together. "You rustle up a pair of old jeans we can cut the leg out of and I'll tell Lita we're going for a ride."

On the drive out to Montoya's in the truck, Brenna could see in the rearview mirror how it rasped Trip that he could neither drive nor ride in front because of his leg cast. She could also tell, from the way his eyes followed her shifting of the gears that he was thinking he'd have to trade the vehicle in for an automatic. He wasn't the automatic type.

But he *would* be able to drive an automatic just fine with his left hand and right leg when the time came. That was a blessing. She wondered if he had considered that particular silver lining for everything it was worth.

Only one week remained before Jamison would remove Trip's casts. Brenna knew that Trip both looked forward to the day and dreaded it. It was simpler right now for him to think of his casts as the most immediate cause of his immobility. When only nerve damage remained as the cause, though, he would have another big adjustment to make. She fervently hoped he'd adjust as well to the limitations that lay ahead as he had to his casts.

She stole fleeting glances at him in the mirror. His left arm lay along the back of the seat. His fingers drummed a ceaseless, restless tattoo. She knew what that meant. He was thinking, worrying, spinning his inner wheels. It broke her heart, at such times, to see this hardy, vigorous man of action prevented from doing so much of what he loved.

He had driven these winding roads and hiked every rugged trail in the surrounding hills. He had lived dangerously in treating such fractious animals as stud horses and breeding bulls. His life had been physically active and professionally satisfying. He had made few compromises in those areas. Until now, few had been necessary.

Now, however, he faced a life altered from the one he had anticipated for himself, a future of reduced physical and professional expectations, a future of compromises.

One day at a time, she told herself, hoping that he would come to adopt that attitude, too. There was always the chance that Jamison's medical prognosis was skewed. Hadn't the doctor already marveled, on the day Trip returned to the hospital for X rays, at how swiftly Trip was mending?

"They must be feeding you right," Jamison had said with a wink at Lita and Brenna, who had closed up shop for a day to drive Trip in for the intensive exam.

Brenna knew it hadn't been good cooking that had nourished Trip as much as being in love and regaining his sexual confidence. He had told her in both words and actions that he had never loved as deeply as he did now, nor been as sexually active as he was now.

That, she reflected, was something to build on as he rebuilt his life. And she had already decided she would be a permanent part of Trip Hart's new life, whatever compromises he might have to face. He wasn't alone in being deeply in love and sexier than ever before. As she dwelled lovingly on that thought, another occurred to her. Hmm. A detour onto a deserted dirt fire road might be one excellent idea after the last field call.

Brenna's lips curved in an optimistic smile as she hit a straight stretch of road and floored the accelerator. She had a plan. Oh, yes. One she would present to Trip after he saw that their relationship could be professional as well as emotional and sexual. A few afternoons of field calls should prime him for it.

At Montoya's, Trip diagnosed and Brenna treated. By the time they left the dairy, he was as eager to move on to the next call as he had been hesitant to embark on the first one. That set the tone for the rest of their successful afternoon together.

And when she steered the truck onto the dirt fire road later, she could see from the sudden, ardent gleam in Trip's eyes that he immediately grasped what was on her mind. The sooner she parked the truck, his look in the rearview mirror said, the better.

He had his jeans unbuttoned when she climbed over the front seat and straddled him.

"My, we're getting dextrous with our left hand, aren't we?" she teased.

"Therapy has its up side," he agreed, deftly unbuttoning the plaid shirt she wore and unclasping her bra. "I'm definitely feeling up right now, in more ways than one."

Brenna tipped his chin to gaze into his eyes. "You liked your change of scene today?"

"More than I thought." Trip raked his hand tenderly through her hair. "I more than like *you*, too. You're really something else, Dr. B. J. Deveney. Just the medicine I seem to need."

"And you're just what *I* need, Dr. Hart. Work with me from now on," she urged softly. "Just take each day as it comes."

"I'll think about it."

"What's to think about? Do you have something better to do with your idle moments?"

"No, but—"

"What better way to spend them, then?"

Trip rolled his eyes and groaned. "How do you talk me into these things?"

"Does that mean you're talked into it?"

"Maybe. We'll see."

"That's no answer."

"'Each day as it comes,'" he reproved, gently turning her own words against her.

"Okay, okay. Just don't say no."

"I know *one* thing I'll never say no to."

"And what might that be?"

"Steaming up the back seat with you."

"Mmm. It *is* getting a trifle warm in here, isn't it?"

"Positively tropical." Trip opened her shirt wide and pushed the cups of her bra aside. "Look at that," he murmured, touching his thumb to the turgid nipple of one breast. "Positively insatiable."

Brenna arched her breasts out to him and threw her head back as Trip squeezed one and then the other in his palm.

"Insatiable, am I? And who's to blame for it but you?"

"Me?" His expression and tone were all mock innocence even as his hand moved with wily intent on her.

"Yes, you." She unbuttoned his shirt and pulled the tails out of his pants. "You're so good at what you do, there's no way I'll ever get enough."

"Get close and I'll do it again," he urged, pulling her forward and circling his tongue around the budded tip of her bare breast.

She moaned as he hungrily sucked her in without ceasing the swirling motion of his tongue. She furrowed her fingers through the hair on his chest and massaged his nipples. Insatiable. She knew he didn't mean it literally. There were times when he left her so replete, she felt certain she'd never build back to needing again. Within hours, though, she was needing what only he could give her. It took a skilled and loving lover to make a woman want him more every time. Trip was that lover.

She felt for the opening of his jeans when he gently scraped her nipples with his teeth, his thumbnail, and whispered how much he loved her, craved her, thought about her day and night.

She found him and gasped. There, oh, there he was. Bursting free at last. Filling her eager hands. Hard and hot and so big, so smooth, so thick, so ready that he was pearled at the tip with moisture. Insatiable? Brenna sighed. So was he. So was he.

His hand molded to the notch of her thighs and stroked her through her slacks, inciting a riot of sensation that made her quake and quiver and know she couldn't wait one more minute to have him inside her, to dissolve his resistance, his reluctance, his doubts. To envelop him in her smoldering heat. To ignite and fuel his hope.

Imperative in her desire, she lifted up, unzipped her slacks, got one leg out of them and her panties and let herself slide down onto him. With little need for restraint now that Trip's ribs were better, she moved as the spirit moved her and let nothing hold her back. Absorbing every thrust of his tongue in her mouth, crushing her breasts into his chest, she pressed her argument home with her body, loving him faster, harder, more feverishly than she had ever done.

He swallowed her helpless scream when she climaxed, then tore his mouth away from hers to watch her face in wonder as the swift, hot jets of his surrender to love and hope shot straight to her core. *"Corazón!"*

11

ON THE FIFTH OF AUGUST, a week after Trip started working occasional office hours and making field calls with Brenna, Lita drove him in to have his casts removed. Brenna was locking up the office at the end of the day when the car turned into the gravel driveway.

"Malia! Byron!" she excitedly called to her two pigs, who were snoozing in the shade of the old oak. "Guess who's home without his casts?"

They both trotted over and waited with her for the car to roll up the long driveway. The late afternoon sun glared on the windshield, but Brenna was able to make out one shape in the driver's seat and another in the passenger seat. No casts. It was hard to believe. And a little scary.

The car pulled to a stop, and Lita got out of the passenger side with Trip's crutch in tow. Brenna caught her breath and watched Lita round the car to the driver's side. Trip had driven home? Of course. Lita's car had an automatic transmission. Trip *had* driven home.

The door on the driver's side swung open. Brenna started walking forward, then broke into a run. Words failed her when she reached the car and saw that he was wearing khaki slacks, a forest-green polo shirt and a vulnerable half smile. Speechless, she stood with Lita and watched him gingerly lift his left leg out of the car with his left hand and settle his foot on the ground. Brenna saw the outline of a leg brace under his pant leg. He swiveled in the car seat and out came his other leg. His right arm was in a sling.

Brenna swallowed hard. He looked pale under the shock of dark red hair that had grown out now to the longish, side-parted style he'd worn before. She held a hand out to him.

Trip shook his head, gripped the top of the car door with his able hand and stood. Lita slipped the crutch under his arm and there he was, more on his own than he had been in weeks.

"Miss me on calls today?" he murmured.

Swallowing back a knot of tears, Brenna nodded. "I missed you all day long."

Lita cleared her throat. "I need to stretch my legs after that long ride. Come, *poquitos*. Let's go see if the blackberries are ripe down by the pump house." Byron and Malia trotted off behind her.

"Well?" Trip said, watching the trio depart. "Aren't you going to say anything?"

"Only that you look almost as good in clothes as you look out of them," said Brenna, almost afraid to touch him.

His smile quivered. "The elbow works, but I can't move any part of my hand."

"And your leg?"

"It bends at the knee, but not on its own. The brace is hinged so I can walk—sort of. Jamison says I can throw away the sling in a couple of days and the crutch in a couple of weeks."

"How was driving?"

His eyes brightened slightly. "The easiest thing I've done in weeks—except for loving you."

"There's something wrong, though. Isn't there?" Brenna pressed a kiss to his lips. "What is it?"

"Everything," he said, his smile fading on a shaky sigh. "You'd think I'd be jumping for joy to be out of plaster, wouldn't you?"

"I think you look wonderful."

"You aren't looking at my arm. Look at it. It looks like an old man's. You don't even want to see my leg, believe me."

"I do, too. Later. After your mother leaves." She curled her hand around his elbow. "Let's go in and have a glass of wine."

"First I want a shower. Do you know how long it's been since I had one?"

Brenna laughed. "Since before I met you, I believe."

He halted halfway to the kitchen door and looked solemnly at her. "Brenna?"

"What?"

"I'm going to have to sell out. That's a fact."

"Not yet. You haven't finished therapy yet. Anything can happen in the next few weeks."

"I'll have to sell," he muttered, his gaze stony. "I knew it the minute my arm came out of the cast. I don't know why I was hoping against hope...letting *you* hope against hope that I'd..."

"Trip, let's talk about it after Lita leaves. In the meantime, kiss me and never forget how much I love you."

They didn't talk about a thing, however, because an emergency call came through before Lita left. A Shetland pony at a distant ranch had come down with a fever and diarrhea. Depressed, and exhausted from a long day, Trip declined to go out on the call with Brenna.

When she returned and slipped into bed with Trip long after midnight, he was sound asleep. She woke before he did and lay watching him. He slept, out of habit now, on his back. His arm was out of the sling, unmoving and pale on top of the covers in contrast to the deep tan his muscular chest and other arm displayed from hours of sunning outside. Therapy would rebuild muscle, she thought, but how much of it?

And what would rebuild his dashed hope, his ravaged confidence? She hadn't realized the extent to which his bulky casts had masked reality. Out of sight, out of mind? Yes, it had been easier to hope with the casts on. Even for her. There was no denying that the sight of his arm was a daunting one. Only the tips of his fingers and thumb had protruded from the cast when it was on, a sight far less distressing than the one Trip faced now.

She could see why his spirits had swung so low the day before, despite his having been able to drive home. It was one thing to stare at a confining cast and hope he could move when it came off. It was something else entirely to stare at his withered hand and not be able to move it with any amount of will or effort.

Brenna knew he had sensation in his hand and arm, because he had always been able to feel the cast around it.

Sensation could exist without mobility, Jamison had explained. At least there was that, she thought. Sensation *was* a wonderful thing, she reminded herself, recalling Trip's touch.

"Not a lot to make a living with, is it?"

So unexpected was his husky murmur that Brenna jumped. The bed jolted. Her eyes jerked from their intent focus on Trip's hand to find his dark gaze on her.

"Sorry to sneak up on you like that," Trip said. "You been awake long?"

"N-no." Brenna drew a deep, calming breath and leaned over to kiss him. "Have you?"

"Long enough to see what you were thinking."

She stroked her hand over his. "Feel that?"

"Yes."

"That's what I was thinking. What a fine thing feeling is." She traced the shape of the fingers he couldn't move and brought them to her lips.

"That's not all you were thinking."

"I know you're disheartened, Trip." Brenna sat up and wrapped the sheet around her against the morning chill. "It took you awhile to get used to the casts. You'll get used to this, too."

"And a few other things, as well," he stated quietly. "I'm finished professionally. It hit me harder yesterday than ever before. Made me wonder what fantasyland I've been living in since I got home. I'll never be what I was."

"I'll never be a partner at the clinic, either."

"You can still practice medicine. That's the bottom line. What in the hell am *I* going to do for a living?"

Marry me. We'll partner the practice together, make a baby or two, live happily ever after. He had never mentioned marriage, though she knew it occupied his thoughts as often as it occupied hers. And as nonstop as that had been, she knew she couldn't say what she'd like to say until Trip knew everything about her—and everything about the plan that was incubating in her mind.

But he was so low right now, she couldn't even begin to broach the subject. *Later,* she told herself for the hundredth time. After intensive therapy. After he bounced back. After he made love to her in all the ravishing ways he had so often and erotically imagined out loud.

"Worry later about making a living," Brenna chided, gently tracing the line of his profile. "You have much more important things to worry about right now."

"Like what?"

"Like whether there's time for a shower for two," she whispered, "before Lita shows up for work."

"A shower," he murmured, pleasantly reminded that he could now take as many as he liked, whenever he liked. With Brenna, if he liked. Brenna, who was rising nude from his big oak bed like Eve before paradise was lost. Brenna, who was ever so slowly playing her hands over her breasts and thighs to tempt him.

A picture formed in his mind of his own hands doing that to her with slippery white soapsuds. Well. There *was* just time enough for what she proposed. And his plastic leg-brace *was* waterproof. And he *was* getting so tempted that Brenna's gaze had already focused on the evidence of his arousal under the covers. Maybe he should put off worrying until a shower for two had been had. Maybe he would. Maybe, hell. He flung off the covers. First things first.

CONRAD ARRIVED right after breakfast, so there was no worrying for Trip until after therapy. Then Brenna needed him in the office to consult on a tricky case of canine hip dysplasia. He ended up staying on to assist in neutering a cat. The cat had no sooner come out of surgery than Dwight dropped in and ended up staying for lunch. After Brenna and Lita ate and returned to the office, Dwight rocked back in his chair and fixed Trip with an uncompromising green stare over his beer can.

"If I don't get to play best man when you marry her, you're dead meat, boy," he drawled.

"I'm halfway there, as it is."

"Not where it counts. A woman doesn't bloom like that if her man's doing anything halfway. You *are* aiming to put a ring on her finger, aren't you?"

Trip shrugged and puffed out a bitter sigh. "I don't know what I'm aiming at other than a new line of work. You wouldn't know anyone who can use a helping hand—just one—would you?"

"Yep. You. Marry Brenna and run this business together. Breed itty-bitty pigs on the side. What have you
got to lose?"

"Just an itty-bitty thing like my self-respect. I can't
have my wife earning my living for me—or making my
child-support payments, for God's sake."

Dwight pursed his lips. "You made Suzanne's living for
her. A lot that gained you in the way of macho pride."

"That's a low blow, lover boy."

"It was aimed at your thick skull. You need some sense
knocked into you, the way you're talking," Dwight retorted.

"I'm thinking straighter than I ever have."

"No, sirree. Not by a mile. Anyone can see Brenna
loves being a vet as much as you do. She'd work even if
she won the biggest lottery in history. Set a date. If you
don't, I'll be next in line to court her."

"Don't you just wish."

Dwight pushed his chair back and stood. "Yep. I'll
wish until you get smart and tell me to rent a tux for your
wedding. Do it, buddy. Life's too short."

"Easy for *you* to say. You wouldn't have to stand by
and watch her baling your hay or shoveling your bull
manure."

"If she laid eyes on me the way she lays eyes on you,
I'd marry her and swallow my pride. You keep thinking
macho, *amigo*, you'll be shooting yourself in your only
good foot."

MACHO. Trip turned the word over and over in his mind
as he drove Lita's car out to Tony Montoya's dairy after
lunch for a courtesy follow-up.

What was macho about wanting to make enough of a
living to live on? It wasn't as if he were insisting on being
lord and master and sole provider. Hell, he'd marry

Brenna in a second if he could be certain of handling half of the work. But he was certain he couldn't. A third of it, maybe. And that only if he got partial movement back in his bad hand and gained right-hand proficiency with his left.

Dammit!

His knuckles whitened in their grip on the steering wheel. How had he gotten so love-dazed in the past few weeks that he'd pushed the hard, cold facts of his future into the farthest corner of his mind? Had he actually spoken the word *nuera* that day to his mother? Love-dazed to the point of total idiocy. And sex-dazed, to boot. Dazed enough to feel a sexual stir, even now, when he recalled how his day had begun.

He scowled at the winding road ahead. So what if he was capable of rendering Brenna limp with ecstasy in bed or shower or kitchen? A good marriage required the mutual respect and admiration of both partners. He should know, having once married a woman too flighty and irresponsible to truly respect. It killed him to imagine Brenna looking upon him as more of a liability than an equal.

He knew how, once a couple settled into a routine, the little things needled up to irritate and undermine. Add a big thing like Brenna shouldering the bulk of the work, pulling in the bulk of the income, and respect and admiration could shrink real quickly into resentment.

He gritted his teeth. Dependent. He despised every letter of the word. That's what he'd be in the last analysis if he took Dwight's advice and ran with it. Easy for Dwight, who was dependent on no one, to say. Macho. Huh.

"WHAT DO YOU THINK of October for the wedding, *amiga*? Everett wants to honeymoon for three weeks in

Europe. Everyone says it's *the* month to go, with good weather and no crowds."

Brenna leaned, chin propped on her hand, against the reception counter in the office and gazed distractedly out the window. "England?" she murmured. "Sounds perfect."

"Close but no *cigarro*," Lita said with a wry smile. "I'm talking Europe, not England, *muchacha*."

Brenna turned to Lita and rolled her eyes in self-reproach. "Sorry, I'm just . . ."

"Tired?"

"Thinking. About you and yoga. When you do it, do you meditate?"

"Would you believe Everett asked me the same thing last night? Of course I do. I always sit in a full lotus position when I finish. I close my eyes and just let myself be for fifteen minutes or so. He had the idea that there was a lot of voodoo hocus-pocus to it. I told him he sounded just like Trip."

Brenna threw her a cautious glance. "You feel normal when you do it?"

"Normal, and very relaxed, and refreshed when I'm through. Why?"

"Just curious. Before I came here, a friend in San Jose suggested I might want to take a class sometime and try it. Where did you learn?"

Lita looked somewhat sheepish. "Through the commune Suzanne joined when it was nearby. They had a wonderful hatha-yoga teacher with them at the beginning, before Suzanne got involved. He gave classes in the village, but went back to India around the time Suzanne took the plunge. He was a true *caballero*, Brenna, not like that *calabaza* Suzanne ran off with. Try to explain the difference to Trip, though. *Ay, Chihuahua.* He lumps it all together, the good and the bad, ever since."

"I know." Brenna pushed off from the counter and gave it a slap. "October in Europe sounds great, Lita. Have you found a wedding dress, yet?"

"Not yet." Lita thought for a minute. "You know, I have an interesting book at home about meditation. It's written by a Harvard M.D. I'll bring it in tomorrow, if you'd like."

Brenna shrugged and tried not to look as interested as she was. "Sure. Why not?"

LITA TOOK THE NEXT SATURDAY off and spent the weekend in San Francisco with Everett to shop for diamonds and a dress. Brenna decided it was as good a weekend as any to tell Trip the whole story of her lost partnership. She had read Lita's book one night in the middle of the week when Trip went over to Dwight's to watch a baseball game on TV.

What the highly respected Harvard doctor had to say was just the scientific reinforcement she needed to propose her plan for the future to Trip. After dinner on Saturday night, she promised herself, she would bite the bullet and tell him all. It might mean the end of everything, but it was something she'd have to risk.

Without Lita in the office on Saturday, Trip and Brenna juggled phones, reception, treatment and one minor surgery. It started out a busy day and didn't let up until just before closing when a gaunt coyote limped into the empty parking lot.

Malia, who was snoozing on the battered leather couch in the reception area, was the first to notice the newcomer through the open door and realize it might be starved for a pork chop. She scrambled for cover behind the reception counter, almost upending Trip, who was on the phone scheduling a Monday appointment. In the dispensary with Brenna, Byron heard the commotion and rushed out to see what was happening. Brenna followed close on his tiny heels.

Trip got off the phone quickly. He and Brenna both stood staring out the door with the pigs huddling at their feet.

"It might be rabid," Trip said. "Put them in the infirmary."

Brenna scooped up a pig under each arm and locked them away.

"Now that I've had a better look, I know that coyote," Trip said when she joined him at the open door. "She tangled with one of Dwight's dogs a year ago."

"Which one?"

"Pirate. The Australian Shepherd. He ripped her left ear back. See how it flops now? I stitched it together. Best I could do. Kept her here until the stitches came out."

"She's bled a lot," Brenna murmured. "Look at her right front shoulder."

"Gunshot, no doubt. She came too close to somebody's livestock. Whoever shot her missed a bull's-eye by an inch."

"I've never handled a coyote before. What about rabies?"

"No problem. I vaccinated her against it before I let her go last year."

"How do we get her in here?"

The question was moot, though. As they watched, the panting animal collapsed flat on her side, a scruffy, unconscious pile of skin and bones.

"Get a muzzle, and ties for her legs," Trip said. "I'll find the stretcher."

With everything they needed, they cautiously approached the coyote. Trip quickly slipped the muzzle over its jaws while Brenna secured its feet. They slid it onto the stretcher. Trip had to crook his elbow under one of the wooden stretcher handles to lift his end, and Brenna saw him grimace with the effort.

She made a mental note to look into attaching straps to the stretcher handles so that he could manage his end more easily in the future. There were so many aspects of the job, outside of actual surgery, that could be easily modified to accommodate his disability. This was just one more.

On the operating table, Trip checked vital signs while Brenna did a manual exam for injuries other than the shoulder wound.

"She's alive, but only by a thread," was Trip's assessment.

Together, he and Brenna scrubbed for surgery, cleaned the coyote's badly infected wound and shaved the area around it.

"I'm surprised Dwight didn't shoot her the day she mixed it up with Pirate," Brenna commented, knowing that ranchers hated the hungry packs of coyotes who often preyed on healthy calves and lambs or those animals who were weak and sick. In the ranching community, the only good coyote was a dead one.

Trip replied, "I was at Dwight's that day, vaccinating his steers, when we heard the squabble and broke it up. He knows me when it comes to any animal that needs medical help. He didn't dare reach for his gun. Pirate came out of the fight without a scratch. I wrestled this feisty little loser down, checked for rabies and patched her up."

"I'll bet Dwight just shook his head."

"Worse than that." Trip chuckled. "Nothing he had to say can be repeated, not even in impolite company."

"Dwight does have a way with a colorful word," Brenna agreed, chuckling, too.

"He called me a new one the other day after lunch," Trip murmured, starting an intravenous solution to replace the coyote's lost body fluids.

"Oh? I didn't know there was an insult you two hadn't already traded at least twice. Is it anything you can repeat in impolite company?"

"How does 'macho' strike you as an insult?"

Brenna raised her eyebrows and flicked off the shaver. "That depends on how he meant it. How did it strike *you*?"

"The wrong way. I'm not pigheaded."

"About what?"

He glanced up from adjusting the drip of the IV. "About anything that really matters. What do you mean 'about what?'"

"Only that I've known you to dig your heels in a little too deeply for your own good, on occasion."

"*Stubborn* and *pigheaded* aren't the same thing."

"Maybe Dwight wasn't making any fine distinctions."

"Oh, he was. Macho. He should talk."

"He must have had his reasons."

"You bet. He said I—" Trip stopped and dropped his gaze. "We were arguing about the lottery."

"What does macho have to do with the lottery?"

"More than you think. Tell me, would you choose to work, even if you won the whole enchilada?"

"Me?" She gave it a moment's thought. "I guess I'd rather be a vet than a millionaire, since I've never bought a lottery ticket."

"You sure about that?"

"Positive." She had a quick mental debate with herself before adding, "Instead of buying lottery tickets, I've saved to buy into a practice."

A long silence held sway before Trip looked up and said in a low voice, "Not this practice."

She met his gaze. "We could do it together, Trip. I know we could."

"It wouldn't be an equal partnership."

"I don't care about that."

"I do."

"Let's at least talk about it after we're through here. Please. There's something else we have to discuss, too." She bit her lip. "Something I haven't told you."

Trip's eyebrows drew together in a puzzled frown. What?"

"It's personal."

"Why haven't you told me?"

"After we're through, Trip. Let's get the bullet out of our friend first."

It happened in the middle of surgery. Brenna had just picked the bullet out when the coyote's heart stopped. She and Trip stared at each other over the animal's inert form, then launched into a tense, concerted effort to resuscitate her.

Nothing worked.

Brenna felt the heat rush through her arms into her hand at the same moment Trip said, "She's gone."

The tingling, the vibration. Brenna caught her breath. It was stronger than ever before. She looked from the coyote to Trip then back at the coyote. Everything began to fade away into a surrounding mist. Everything but herself and the animal on the surgery table. Her ears rang for a moment and then a great calm descended on her, even as heat suffused her hands and seemed to pour out of them.

"No..." Brenna placed her hand on the coyote's head. "She's not gone, yet. No..." She placed her other hand on the scruffy fur of the coyote's flank and closed her eyes.

"Brenna, she's dead. What are you doing?"

Trip's voice came to her as if from a great distance. Her answering whisper sounded lighter than air.

"Don't touch me. Don't touch her."

"Brenna?"

She didn't answer. Couldn't answer. She just let go and let the energy pour through her into the frail body under her hands.

"Brenna, what do you—"

She felt the coyote jerk once, twice, then draw a huge shuddering breath.

As quickly as it had come, the energy deserted, leaving Brenna disoriented for a moment after she opened her eyes. She shook her head to clear it and lifted her hands from the coyote, whose audible breathing was as steady and strong as she knew its pulse now was.

Brenna looked up from the operating table to the man on the other side of it. He was staring at her, his mouth open, his face pale.

"That's what I haven't told you, Trip."

12

TRIP OPENED HIS MOUTH to say something, then shut it and shifted his dumbfounded stare from Brenna to the coyote on the operating table.

"She was gone! I saw it with my own—" His eyes returned to Brenna. "What did you do?"

"I'll explain after we're through and she's in recovery."

He shook his head. His eyes darkened. "I don't believe this. What did you do?"

"Trip, we have to close her up. Let's concentrate on that right now."

Trip clamped his lips together and passed her a suture. Every few stitches, Brenna glanced at his face. His brows were locked in a dark frown. With perfect precision, he passed her each instrument she required, at the precise moment it was required. Not a word was spoken. No sooner did she knot a stitch than he snipped it.

There might have been no tension crackling between them, so perfect was their synchrony in surgery. As perfect as when they made love together, she thought with a pang. Had last night been the last time? Her hand trembled as she tied her last perfect stitch.

When they were through, she stripped off her surgical gloves and said, "I'll get the dinner started while you wait for her to come around."

He nodded, his frown firmly locked in place.

A little later, Trip came in and found Brenna at the sink, scraping carrots and potatoes.

"She's groggy but coming along," he said, going to the refrigerator. "Want a beer?"

"No, thanks."

Trip pulled one out, sat at the table and popped the top. "I'm listening," he said gruffly.

Brenna dried her hands, pulled out a chair and sat across from him.

"I—" She stopped and took a deep breath for the plunge. "I know you have strong feelings about what I haven't told you, Trip."

"Which is?"

"I'm what they call a healer."

His dark gaze on her was wary. He made the word sound preposterous when he repeated after her, "A healer."

"Yes, I—this thing happens to me every so often—to my hands, I mean." She laid them palms up on the red-checked tablecloth. "Feel them right now."

Trip snapped his head back an inch as if she had suddenly become infectious. "I'm still listening."

Brenna's heart sank. He wouldn't touch what for weeks he had touched at every opportunity, what had touched him in every loving and intimate way known to woman and man. Not now. Rational, logical, proof oriented, he refused to reach out and prove to himself how little he had to fear. Oh, he was listening all right. But not in the open, nonjudgmental way she needed. Neither had her ex-colleagues listened in that way when she had tried to explain the same thing to them.

"Right now they're just like they always are, except when it happens."

"When what happens?"

"Heat and tingling. It's an energy that rushes into my hands." She lifted her shoulders in appeal. "Something happens to the animal I'm working on at that moment.

I've seen tumors disappear or shrink shortly after that. Wounds will sometimes take only half the normal time to heal. More often it just calms a stressed animal so that it willingly accepts treatment."

Trip pursed his lips. "Like Trixie."

Brenna nodded. "Exactly like that. I never know when it's going to come through—it just comes. It's been that way ever since it started over a year ago. I had a few sessions with another healer before I—"

"Hold it. You're in cahoots with someone else on this?"

"No. I just met with her a few times to find out what was happening to me. My psychiatrist recommended her."

Trip pushed his chair back. "You have a shrink?"

"*Had* a shrink. My medical doctor referred me to him. He said I was normal mentally and emotionally and there was nothing he could do. Howmedica was being tested at Stanford and—"

"Howmedica?" Trip rolled his eyes and stood up. "I've heard enough."

"Sit down, Trip. I'm not finished. Howmedica Plant is not a weirdo or a wacko or anything else her unusual name might imply. It's her birth name, and she's a very gifted psychic who can not only see human auras, but—"

"Save the buts," said Trip, who stayed on his feet. "I've sat and listened to enough of this weirdo, wacko, new-age crap already from Suzanne. Psychics. Human auras. Crystal healing. Chanting. Channeling. Past lives. Life after death. Soul mates. Subliminal tapes. Prosperity programming. Horoscopes. Mantras. What's *your* mantra, by the way?"

Brenna stood, her hands balled into fists at her side. "I don't have one. Yet."

"Not contemplating your beingness yet?" he inquired with raised eyebrows. "After a few more sessions with Howmedica Tree you *will* be."

"Plant. Her last name is Plant."

"Tree, Shrub, that's the way it goes with that grubby pack of leeches. They sucked Suzanne and her money— *my* money—in with their brainwashing, and before I could say deprogram she was history and so was my kid."

"Trip, I was hoping we could discuss this rationally."

"Never try to apply the rational to the irrational with me, Brenna. I get a nice, clear picture of what we're discussing here. You think you're a healer—"

"I don't think so, I *know* it. You saw the evidence."

"Maybe I did. Maybe I didn't. Maybe there was just enough of a survival instinct in that coyote that she came back from the brink."

"Explain Trixie, then."

"Maybe she likes women better than she likes Ash Pemberton or Trip Hart."

"Maybe you're grasping at straws. I have other witnesses. The vets at the clinic didn't blackball me after six years for nothing. They saw it, too, and feared it just as much as you're fearing it now. Be reasonable, Trip. Nature isn't as rational as you prefer to think. The scientists studying Howmedica are simply trying to understand and explain what happens."

Trip grabbed his beer from the table and took a swig. "A lot of things happen in this world," he said bitterly. "A tree blows down in a brushfire and ends a man's career. A relief vet blows in from San Jose and turns a man's head with her talk of hope and love and creative bedtimes. Only it turns out she's tuned in to the same loony wavelength as his ex-wife is. I lost a wife and a daughter to the new age, *señorita*, and I'm not volunteering again."

"Trip, I'm not Suzanne. I didn't seek out what happened to me. All I want is to practice medicine out here with you and do what I can to understand and develop the gift I have. The better I do that, the better I can help animals."

"Not the animals in *my* practice," Trip retorted.

"You'd rather have seen that coyote die, Trip? You who weren't willing to let a deer die in a fire? I'm not buying that argument for one second. And I'm not saying trust everything to hands-on healing, but I *am* saying it can and should be used along with traditional techniques."

"Go back to San Jose, Brenna," Trip said, wearily shaking his head. "I'll stick to the good old earthbound medicine I know, thank you very much."

"You'll stick to nothing if you sell out. Without me, you'll have to sell." She stopped, realizing the inadvertent cruelty in what she'd said. "I'm sorry. I didn't mean to—"

"Rub it in?" he interjected. "I can take it. But before you rub more salt in that particular wound, let me do a little rubbing in of my own."

"Trip, I—"

"If you're a bona fide healer, explain why you haven't healed *me*. Why am I dragging a dead hand and leg around, if you're so gifted?"

"It only happens with animals—except for your burns. That's all I know. The only other thing I know is I love you. You love me. We've never been happier in our lives than we've been together. Why throw that away over this?"

"Stop the healing and tingling and wanting to know more, and we won't have to throw anything away."

"Stop it?" Brenna blinked in disbelief. "Just like that? You *are* blind. I can no more stop what I didn't start than you can do surgery at will with your right hand."

"Keep rubbing it in, Brenna, and I'll help you pack those bags. Like I said, one wife, one daughter is all I ever need to lose."

Brenna gritted her teeth. "According to the gossip mill in these parts, your marriage was on the rocks from the start. The way I hear it—and I didn't ask—you didn't lose much in the way of a wife. You told me yourself it was losing Aura that broke your heart."

"Aura," Trip muttered. "I should have known what was going on when Suzanne insisted on naming her that. Talk about blind. She was sneaking off to that goofy commune long before she started lugging the books and tapes and magic crystals home trying to convert me."

"How can you even begin to compare me to Suzanne? I'm no flighty airhead chasing the latest new-age fad. She never fit into your world and I do. She wasn't a healer."

"She wanted to be. That and a lot of other things. Her damned guru claimed he could teach Suzanne to heal, for a fee. Always a fee. You'll see when you start getting sucked in. You'd be better off buying lottery tickets."

"As a sane, balanced human being with something worthwhile to explore, I'll take my chances, Trip."

Trip moved to the screen door and shouldered it half open. "It was fun while it lasted, *corazón*, but *adiós* and *vaya con Dios*. I'll go check on the miracle in the infirmary and write your final paycheck while I'm at it. You can head out now and be home for supper."

"Trip…" Brenna's eyes filled with tears. "We're so good together. We can't let it end like this, in a standoff over what's rational and what's not."

His mouth hardened into a line that banished every trace of the dimple Brenna adored. "Maybe you can't, but I can. Twice burned, more than twice shy."

"You got burned once. I got burned once. We both married flakes. Don't make it sound worse than it was."

"I'm not. It's more truth than rumor that Suzanne and I were a mismatch from the day we met. She suckered me and I was mistaken enough about her to get suckered. But I got burned again when she took Aura," he stated, his tone flat and final.

"What about the children you and I could have, Trip?"

He shouldered all the way through the screen door and looked back one last time. His face was harsh, uncompromising, his eyes dark with pain. Then he turned and limped out without a further word.

13

INDIAN SUMMER. It had begun, hot and dry, right after a drizzly Labor Day and still reigned supreme on Saturday the first of October. It was so hot in San Jose that Byron and Malia insisted on holing up in the air-conditioned house rather than lolling in their wading pool outside. Like children cooped up on a bad-weather day, they were antsy.

"No, we are not going to play another game of hide-and-seek," Brenna said, refusing to meet the two pairs of wistful eyes that begged her to put her magazine down and get up from where she lay on the couch for just one more game.

Byron stretched out on his tummy on the beige shag carpet, rested his chin on his little front hooves and let out a strangled, frustrated sigh. Malia did the same with a sigh twice as loud as Byron's.

"Sorry, kids. As soon as I finish this short story, I'm going to nod off on this very spot and nap the afternoon away. The phone is staying unplugged all day and so am I. After three late shifts at the all-night clinic and four games of hide-and-seek, I've had it."

That was an understatement. Brenna had more than had it. Nothing seemed to ease the pain. Nothing had ever hurt as deeply as her loss of Trip's love. Not Fletcher's lechery. Not being blackballed at the clinic. Nothing.

Brenna shoved the magazine onto the coffee table and closed her eyes. Sleep. If only she could do it without dreaming of Trip making hot, heady love to her in his big oak bed. If only she could sleep without crying her eyes out first. If only...

The past two months had been an eternity of *if only*s. She hated to think of how long it would take for a year to pass at that rate. Or how long it would take for the pain to ebb away. Working herself to the brink of exhaustion with relief work didn't help. Nothing helped. Not even her weekly study sessions with Howmedica.

If only Trip had been able to see reason. If only he hadn't written that final paycheck and handed it to her without a word before she left. In return she had slapped the Harvard physician's book on meditation onto his desk and said, "Try reading it with an open mind—if you can."

Two heavy sighs emanated again from the two on the carpet.

"No, no, and no," Brenna told them with a catch in her voice at how much like Trip she sounded saying that word.

"No," he had replied in answer to her final plea for him to think twice before she drove back to San Jose. "It's over, Brenna. Over."

A month later she had seen his classified ad listed in a veterinary news magazine under Practices For Sale. That was that—except for two greeting cards from San Luis Obispo that said only, "I'm praying, *amiga*. Love, Lita."

All Brenna had done or could do was wonder. Wonder if he had hired another relief vet to keep things going until a sale came through. Wonder if the coyote had survived. Wonder if Lita had found the perfect dress. Wonder if she and Everett had set a date. Wonder if Trip had even opened the book. Wonder if he ever reached for her in his sleep and woke with only an aching emptiness in his heart. Wonder and hurt. Hurt and wonder.

She squeezed her eyes tighter shut and pinched the bridge of her nose between thumb and forefinger. She would not cry. Not today. Every day she told herself that, and every day, at some point, the tears spilled over. She pinched harder. Not today. If she could just get through one whole day without them, a second day without tears might be possible.

Hot and bitter, they gathered behind her eyes. She pulled a tissue from the pocket of the faded cutoffs she wore and blew her nose. Today wouldn't be the day. She wiped her eyes and blew again. Maybe tomorrow.

By then, though, she'd have slept and dreamed and wakened with an aching heart and body all over again. She hadn't known a woman could miss a man's kiss, his touch, his every expression of love so much. If only he hadn't been the intense and passionate lover that he'd been. If only she could forget every shape and texture of his body, every touch of his lips to her, every sweet morning, noon and midnight they'd spent making love.

That morning in the shower. She almost whimpered now, remembering how Trip had soaped her breasts, circled the slick surface of the fragrant soap bar over her water-glistened nipples, stroked the long edge of it between her legs, uttered throaty, primal words of intent as he backed her against the steamed tiles, hooked his hand behind her knee and slowly lifted her leg until she was wide open to his probing tip and extending her own primal invitation for him to pin her to the shower wall.

A knock on the door sent Byron and Malia shooting to their feet. The strangled, frustrated sigh this time was Brenna's. Every day for the past week, someone or something had knocked on her door at precisely the wrong moment. Yesterday it had been a junior-high student selling tickets to a class play. The day before that it had been her next-door neighbor asking to borrow her lawn mower because his had gone on the blink in the middle of his front lawn. Three days ago it had been a misguided woodpecker.

She blew her nose one last time and rose from the couch, hiking up her cutoffs and smoothing her stretchy yellow tube top over her breasts. Putting her eye to the peephole, she caught her breath and snapped back.

It couldn't be!

Eye to the peephole again, she saw that it was. Trip Hart. In the flesh. Inches away. Wearing what looked like . . . a black tuxedo?

Trip. Brenna stepped back, swallowed hard and pressed her suddenly damp palms together. Trip. What did he want? Why was he here?

He knocked again. She unlocked and opened the door.

Trip backed out to the very edge of the front step and swallowed hard. Never had he seen Brenna more beautiful than she seemed to him in that moment. Every silky strand of light brown hair, every pinpoint freckle, every delicate toe of her bare feet, every tear trembling in her sherry-amber eyes was beauty incarnate.

They might have stood staring forever, transfixed, had Byron and Malia not catapulted past Brenna and flung themselves against Trip's long legs, squealing and grunting the most overjoyed of welcomes.

"Hi, guys," he said, kneeling to scratch them behind the ears with his left hand until they both settled for just wagging their tiny pigtails as fast as they could to express their joy. "How about a game of hide-and-seek? Go hide. We'll be along in a couple of minutes. Ten. Nine. Eight . . ."

Off they raced to hide themselves away.

Two huge tears wobbled in Brenna's eyes at this scene she had never imagined she'd witness again.

Trip looked up at her and slowly stood. "I tried to call but no answer. Thought I'd drive by on the off chance you might be somewhere around."

"Why—" Brenna cleared her throat. "Why the tux?"

"Mom and Ev are getting married in a couple of hours."

"Where?"

"Here in San Jose. A lot of Ev's family live north of San Francisco. This was a good middle spot. The reception's at the San Jose Fairmont. Half the county's here—my sisters and Aura, too. Would you come and watch me give Mom away?"

"Trip, I—"

"She'll barely speak to me, even on her wedding day." Brenna's chin quivered. "You said it was over. Is it?"

"No. Dwight was right," he said, his dark eyes hot, anguished, pleading. "I've been a stubborn, thick-headed, macho bastard. I'm sorry. I can't tell you how sorry. I love you, *corazón*. I need you in my life. I can't help it, can't fight it one more day."

"What about the way I am? Did you read the book?"

He nodded. "Yesterday. I didn't really need to, though. I know you're not the type to go off the deep end like Suzanne did. What's happened to you has happened, period. It deserves exploring. If meditation will help, so be it. Applying my own sane, rational logic to the subject helped me decide."

"Decide what?" Brenna held her breath.

"That your gift of healing is no different from the gift of love. Science can't put love in a test tube and prove its existence, yet it exists. So does the healing in your hands. Love grows when it's nurtured and so will your gift if you nurture it. Perfectly logical."

Brenna took a tentative step forward, but Trip held up a hand to halt her. "I haven't changed otherwise, Brenna.

I'm stuck with a leg brace for life and though my arm's back to normal, my hand hasn't responded to therapy. The nerves are shot. I'll never do surgery again."

Brenna's face fell. "Don't tell me you sold the practice. Please."

"I almost did, but not quite. I pulled the listing at the last minute yesterday."

"You mean we can still..." She took a hopeful step forward.

He stood firm. "One hand is the most I'll ever be able to lend you if we work together."

"*When* we work together, Trip."

"My leg and hand aren't my only disabilities," he murmured, stepping inside. "You wouldn't know a cure for a broken heart, would you, *corazón*?"

Brenna smiled through her tears. "Only one. The cure for mine just walked in the door."

From their seat on the couch, Byron and Malia watched their dashing new master sweep their tearful mistress up in his arms and limp into the bedroom at the end of the hall.

Then, polite little creatures that they were, they averted their gazes from the open bedchamber door and grinned from ear to ear. *Home safe!*

This month's
irresistible novels from

— TEMPTATION —

JUST JAKE by Shirley Larson

Alexandra Holden was on the verge of success selling her
property in the Florida Keys. All she had to do was evict
the sexy and distracting Jake Hustead . . .

TEMPERATURE'S RISING by Susan Gayle

Nurse Kyla Bradford knew Ted Spencer wasn't sick the
moment she encountered him. He was trying to fake his
way into Emergency to get the scoop on the hospital's
latest controversy. She would have to teach him a lesson.

CHEAP THRILLS by Tiffany White

He was no Peeping Tom: Crew Harper was just doing
his job – outside the fourth storey of an office block. But
a movement through the window caught his eye – Alexia
Grant was undressing!

THE MAGIC TOUCH by Roseanne Williams

When Brenna Deveney signed on as relief veterinarian
for the injured and bedridden Dr Trip Hart, she had no
idea she would be tending the sexy bachelor along with
the other animals.

Spoil yourself next month
with these four novels from

— TEMPTATION —

THE DREAM by Barbara Delinsky
(First in a stirring new trilogy)

The sexy, enigmatic Carter Malloy was the one man
Jessica Crosslyn had spent her life trying to avoid. But
if she wanted to save her home, Crosslyn Rise, she would
have to place her entire future in Carter's hands.

TALISMAN by Laurien Berenson

Kelly Ransome had been hired to train Eric Devane's
dog, but she soon found it was Eric who needed
obedience lessons. He just wouldn't take *no* for an
answer!

THE PERFECT MATE by Eugenia Riley

Susan Nowotny was in serious trouble. Her brother's
gambling had cost her a few dollars over the years – now
it was about to cost her her life. Eligible, sexy, *wealthy*
Ben Adams was her last resort.

MY FAIR BABY by Carin Rafferty

If Erica Stewart didn't agree to let her little boy appear
in his ad company's latest commercials, Alex Harte
would lose a key account. How could he secure this
stubborn woman's consent?

Relax in the sun with our Summer Reading Selection

Four new Romances by favourite authors, Anne Beaumont, Sandra Marton, Susan Napier and Yvonne Whittal, have been specially chosen by Mills & Boon to help you escape from it all this Summer.

Price: £5.80. Published: July 1991

Available from Boots, Martins, John Menzies, W.H. Smith, Woolworths and other paperback stockists.

Also available from Mills and Boon Reader Service, P.O. Box 236, Thornton Road, Croydon, Surrey CR9 3RU.